I0618533

Happiness Was Our Reward

By Will Rogers Jr

Will Rogers Jr Publishing

Copyright©2006 All Rights Reserved

ISBN: 978-0-6151-3839-8

Disclaimer:

All persons, events, and institutions in this book are completely fictional and the product of the author's imagination. Any resemblance to actual persons, places, or events is purely coincidental.

Cover art was created by Omar Franco. Visit his website at http://www.mediatconline.com

Table of Contents

Preface

This story was born partially out of the experiences that I have had within the hyper-fundamentalist movement. Although the entire story is fictional, my own experiences contributed in some small measure to those experienced by the characters within the book. The entire book is a work of fiction, although it may seem to some that these experiences have actually happened. What makes the story so compelling is that this type of behavior is actually exhibited within the confines of some Independent Baptist colleges. None of the people in this book are real, but their story nonetheless will strike a chord with those who have experience with these types of colleges and churches.

I have no axe to grind with Independent Fundamental Baptist. I am an IFB, and I attend an IFB church. I do however have a desire to expose the pulpit bullies who use their position of power to build their own corrupt empire. There are many who have been hurt by similiar experiences, and it is my hope and prayer that they will allow God to heal them of the hurts they have suffered.

This book is dedicated to the ones who have been wounded in the name of God by the power-hungry despots who reign within certain circles of the church. It is my prayer that you allow God to work in your lives and heal you of the pain you carry. May the road you travel be easy to walk.

But whoso shall offend one of these little ones which believe in me, it were better for him that a millstone were hanged about his neck, and that he were drowned in the depth of the sea. (Matthew 18:6)

Introduction

Welcome to the world of Jason Lyle Tate. Jason Tate is the son of an Independent Fundamental Baptist preacher. For those of you who are unfamiliar with Independent Fundamental Baptists, I will attempt to explain to you the culture in which these characters live.

Independent Fundamental Baptists(IFB's) are free of any hierarchy as a denomination. Rightly, the IFB movement can't be considered a denomination since each church is totally autonomous from any other church. That is to say, that there is no governing body over the local church. Critics of IFB's point out that this can be destructive, and can give rise to predator pastors who use the pulpit to bully others. Proponents of the IFB movement point out that this also can keep conservative churches from being associated with liberal churches, since they are independent.

IFB churches aren't always as independent as they think however. Certain churches and colleges become well known in the IFB movement, and can create a loyal legion of followers who adhere to the school and church. Even though these other churches are officially independent of the church which they so greatly respect and admire, they often only allow speakers who are for that particular church or college. This has resulted in several "circles" which exist in the world of Independent Baptists.

In the world of IFB's, the pastor of any particular church is seen as the sole head of the church. Some of these pastors demand that their congregants allow the pastor veto power in their lives. If a church member wants to move, or otherwise make a life-changing decision, permission from the pastor must be sought.

In cases where a member leaves this type of church without the pastor's blessing, they may be shunned. In cases where a member exposes gross sin in the life of the pastor or other church leadership or someone loyal to the pastor, that member is ostracized, and sometimes preaches against from the pulpit. This culture of corruption can devastate a person who is unprepared to handle the consequences of such action.

Most IFB churches require the use of only the King James Version of the Bible. Some churches have taken the position that a person can only be saved through the King James Bible. A good majority believe that the King James Bible is a perfect translation, while a small minority of these believes that the King James Version actually corrects the original manuscripts.

In IFB churches, hymns compose most of the music sung. Very rarely do IFB churches use Contemporary Christian Music, because of its association with rock music. Drums are seen by some as an instrument of the devil. Secular music is largely shunned, with the exceptions of classical music such as Beethoven's symphonies.

Many IFB churches view women wearing pants as sinful, and believe women should only wear skirts or dresses. Men are forbidden from wearing necklaces or earrings because they are considered women's attire and thus effeminate.

IFB churches don't allow women to hold any church office, other than Sunday School teacher or secretary. Some preachers and leaders in the IFB movement teach that a wife or girlfriend should not defeat her husband or boyfriend in any type of activity. It is seen as unladylike to defeat a man in any type of activity. Traditional gender roles are encouraged and taught.

Visiting a movie theater is seen by some as a sinful activity. However, renting a movie to watch on one's own television set is not seen as sinful, unless the movie is considered wrong. The right or wrong of a particular movie can change at the whim of the pastor. The types that are mostly preached against are movies with sex scenes or nudity.

Many IFB churches are very aggressive in evangelism. Street preaching takes place to a small extent, but most often door-to-door Soulwinning and handing out tracts are the biggest parts of evangelism in IFB churches. Bus Ministries, in which a bus goes around different parts of town to pick up mainly children for church, are heavily promoted as well. Most Bus Ministries put the kids from the Bus Ministry in a different class than the kids who come from the church itself.

Several large IFB churches throughout the nation have started their own colleges. These colleges are normally unaccredited, since IFB's fear government intrusion into how their school is run and what they can teach. Many of these schools are comparable to a vocational school, because they prefer practical training to theological training. These colleges tend to result in a lot of "inbreeding," because the school will hire their own graduates as faculty and staff members. This tends to create an atmosphere of absolute loyalty to the pastor, who is often the head of the college. Any dissent within the college can result in an immediate firing of a staff member, or expulsion of a student.

Rules are often applied unevenly. Where the average student may be disciplined for a certain infraction, the child of a faculty member may get by with a slap on the wrist or less.

Outsiders are viewed with distrust in the IFB culture, particularly those who are members of other denominations. IFB's take great pride in the notion that they are the only true church, and look with disdain on other churches. Members of other churches may be viewed as either unsaved, babes in Christ, or not right with God. Members of IFB churches who leave may be viewed as bitter or backslidden.

The above can be descriptive of IFB's everywhere to one extent or another. IFB's that hold to all of these distinctives are called "IFBx"(Independent Fundamental Baptist Extreme) by outsiders. While there are many very good, sincere Christians in the IFB movement, there are some very bad ones who have infiltrated the movement and have caused much harm to the body of Christ.

It is the opinion of the author of this story that churches and colleges like the ones described within the story are dangerous not only to Independent Baptist churches and congregations, but also to individual Christians. Some Christians have sadly been crushed under the corrupt influence pictured here. Independent Baptists are for the most part good people, striving to serve God and live their life in a manner pleasing to God. There is a tendency to throw out the entire barrel of apples because of a few bad ones, and it is the hope of this author that the entirety of Independent Baptists are not dismissed by others because of the few bad apples that control a pulpit.

This is the culture that our characters live in. It is a culture that has them warily looking over their shoulder, and watching every step they take. The fear that they could be ripped apart by those in authority is very real to them. For Jason, it's the only life he's ever known. And for him to leave it, those he knows and loves will turn their back on him. But to stay would mean losing the only love he's ever had. He is torn between two worlds, and the knowledge of how to escape it is one he must learn on his own.

Christina is head over heels in love with Jason, and would follow him to the ends of the world. But this is not the only life she's ever known, and she's not as torn between staying there as Jason. She wishes only to be with Jason, but she has to fight all the powers that be for his love.

This is the story of a clash of wills. Who will win, and where Jason ultimately decides to place his heart is a story that while purely fictional, is based in real life practices of IFBx pastors and colleges. Turn the page, and let the journey begin.

Chapter One:

Away From Home

The parking lot of Tennessee Baptist Bible College was abuzz with excitement on that warm day. I could feel the thrill of all the new students as I pulled back onto campus. All the freshmen were lined up on the other side of the parking lot getting their room assignments, and all the other information they needed on getting class schedules. Since I was a returning student, I was able to go through the express lane. I walked over toward the returning student area, where everybody was catching up on events that took place over the summer. As I walked over, I thought back over the previous year's events.

I was the son of a Baptist preacher. To be specific, my dad was an Independent Fundamental Baptist preacher. He pastored a fairly large church, and was in demand for speaking events all across the country. I suppose in some ways, I had gone to college because it was expected of me. I didn't mind all that much, because I was anxious to get away from home. My first month there, I got saved for real during a chapel service. I knew I had never been saved before, and this time, I made it real in my own life. My dad just said that I got my assurance, but I knew in my heart that it had been the real deal.

When I had gone home over the summer, I had found an interesting website online. It was an unofficial website of the college I had attended. Some of the people there were graduates or former attendees of the college, or of Memphis Metro Baptist Church. Others were like-minded Baptists who knew of the church and college, and wanted to talk with those who had gone there. Still others were former Fundamental Baptists who had left the Independent Baptist movement and were now Southern Baptist or Reformed Baptists.

At first, I had vehemently opposed what I thought were the evils of Calvinism. Like any good Independent Baptist preacher boy, I knew all the party lines and talking points, and I stuck with them for a while. But then I honestly started looking at the verses. My opinion had begun to change. I read up on Spurgeon, and what he had taught. It was so different and foreign to my way of thinking. I had always been taught that Calvinists were lazy Christians and poor soulwinners, that is, if they were even saved. But by now, this strange doctrine had taken hold in my heart. It made sense to me, and it actually made the Bible come to light in a way I had never seen before. But I kept my views to myself. There was nobody I could trust with the information that I was a Calvinist. To say it aloud could spell my doom. What would happen if word got out I was a Calvinist? The mere thought sent chills down my spine. But I pushed the thoughts out of my mind, today was a day for seeing friends from the year before. A sudden shout startled me from my thoughts.

"Hey Jason!" Dave yelled to me from across the parking lot.

"Hey Dave! Good to see you! How've you been?"

"Not bad bro, how 'bout yourself?"

"Pretty good," I responded honestly, "it's been a good summer."

"It'll be an even better school year," he said with a grin, "this year you have one up on the Frogs. Now we can have some fun with them together."

I smiled to myself. At TBBC, we called the freshmen "frogs." I'm not really sure why, other than it was just tradition. The way it worked there, frogs were the lowest on the totem pole, unless somebody did something really stupid. Those who were upperclassmen had a big advantage over the freshmen, and could even tell them to do things for them. Dave and I walked through the line, and got our room information.

"I'm on Joshua Two," said Dave looking over his papers, "how about you?"

"Joshua Two, room 131."

"Cool, we're right next door to each other, I'm 133."

"I guess we should head up, and mark our territory before the frogs get there."

We grabbed our stuff out of our cars and walked up into our dorm hall to the second floor, talking as we went. Dave had spent the summer working on his dad's construction crew. Dave was one of the few guys at TBBC who didn't have a dad in the ministry. Some of the other fellows looked down on him for that, but Dave was a great guy to hang out with. I didn't care what his dad did, and it didn't have any bearing on the matter. Dave and I were both studying pastoral theology together, sometimes I'd help him on some things that seemed pretty basic to me, but I always remembered that Dave didn't have the advantage of having a preacher for a dad. Sometimes I looked at having a preacher for a dad as a disadvantage, but when it came to classes, it was pretty helpful.

We decided to stop by my room first, since we would come there first. I opened the door, and saw two freshmen already getting settled in. The rooms were small, but for the guys, each room could hold up to six guys with bunk beds, and had one table, one chair, some small bookshelves, and three small dressers with small closets on top. The freshmen were both taking the bed in the back corner, a bed I knew I wanted and one of the other upperclassmen would want too. Being in the back of the room would afford me more freedom in a way. For one, I would be further from the door, and so didn't have to answer the door if someone knocked. And if someone came in trying to play a practical joke, they were less likely to pick the back bunk for their prank.

"Hey guys," I said nonchalantly "the back bunk is for upperclassmen."

The taller one protested, "But we were here first."

The statement surprised me. Freshmen didn't talk back to upperclassmen, that's the way it was. I decided to quickly put him in his place. I had Dave to back me up if I needed, but I didn't think I would.

"Doesn't matter, upperclassmen get their choice of beds. You guys can take one of the beds by the door."

The dismay on their faces was apparent. They had probably wanted the back beds because they would be closer to the window. Sure that was a nice feature in the summer, but in the winter it got a little cold. The only good thing about it was the distance from the door. I smiled inwardly as I saw them grab their stuff and move toward the bunks by the door. The taller one looked quite upset about the matter. I decided I'd best keep an eye on him. I started putting my stuff up, while Dave helped me. I turned and looked toward the two again, and decided I should at least get their names.

"So who are you guys? I'm Jason Tate." I stuck my hand out as a friendly gesture.

The shorter one grabbed my hand first, "I'm Kyle, Kyle Tanner" he said with a smile. He looked really good-natured.

The taller one looked at me for a moment, then shook my hand, "I'm Adam Quinn."

"Where are you guys from?" I asked.

"We're both from Maryland, Grace Baptist in Silver Springs"

15

replied Adam.

"So your pastor is Tom Burnett?"

"Yes, that's him."

Tom Burnett was a familiar name to me. He'd been to my church a few times to preach, and he and my dad had preached together at conferences all around America. They had both graduated from TBBC, and had gone bus calling together a lot. I decided it would be in my own best interest not to hassle these guys too much yet, until I had a handle on them. Dave and I finished putting my stuff up, and turned and headed for his room.

We walked out of my room, and standing there was Tony. Tony Asperger had been in Dave's room the year before. We were all sophomores together, and knew each other fairly well.

"Hey Dave, what room ya in this year?"

"One-thirty-three, how 'bout you?"

"One-thirty-seven, I'm one of the lucky ones," he said with a sly grin.

We all knew what that meant, his room was going to be less monitored than the others, because it had a dorm supervisor living in it. Dorm supervisors were older students who had been promoted, and basically made sure that the dorms were kept clean and orderly, and everybody woke up on time. But generally, a dorm sup had a lot of freedom in their own room. Their rooms tended to get passed over on the white glove inspections. How lucky is that, I thought to myself? And here I am stuck with two frogs who might try and get uppity with me. I'll admit, I was less than thrilled about having to room with freshmen. Granted, I had been one last year, but still. It wasn't going to be much fun, and I'd have to teach them the ropes. I guess that's why most of the juniors and seniors get the two other male dorm halls, so they don't have to be pestered by the freshmen.

We all grabbed Dave's stuff, and helped him put it up. Tony decided that we should grab some other guys, and run off campus for lunch. Officially, we weren't there yet, so we could run off campus and grab something to eat without having to sign out. We walked upstairs, and found Brian Whitehead, and Michael Quinn, two other sophomores, and went out to Tony's car. Tony had a large Buick his grandfather had given him for college, and it would hold a pretty large number of guys, perfect for running down to a local restaurant. We headed down to Pizza Time, a local pizza parlor ran by an Italian family. We sat and swapped summer stories as we ate our pizza. We had a few good laughs, then ordered a couple of extra pizzas to take back to the dorm and torture the frogs with.

We pulled back into the parking lot, and parked right over by our dorm. Since it was still the first day of getting set up, we were allowed on other dorm floors, so Brian and Michael came downstairs with us. By this time, most of the others had gotten there, and the hall was full of frogs. We all looked at each other, a bit dismayed at the thought of sharing an entire dorm with freshmen.

"Hey, is that pizza?" Kyle saw the boxes and was practically salivating at the sight.

"Sure is," said Tony, "just picked it up."

Dave and I sat down on the bench in the hall, and the others sat down with us, and Tony started handing out some slices to all of the sophomores. Just then, Jacob came down the stairs. Jacob Hall was the

17

dorm sup this year, Tony turned and grinned.

"Hey Jake, want some pizza?"

"Hey guys, sure, what ya got?"

"Got one supreme, and one all meats."

Jake grabbed a slice, and sat down with us and we all started talking. Jake was pretty cool, his dad was on staff at the college, which was how he wound up a dorm sup. We relaxed, but I knew we were still being watched by the frogs. I turned, and saw Kyle staring at us.

"Yes?" I said looking at him, "Can I help you?"

The other guys all looked up at Kyle. "Can I have a slice?" he asked.

"Nope," said Michael, "don't have enough, sorry."

I could see the disappointment on his face, and felt a brief pang of guilt. I remembered all too well what it was like to be a frog, and be left out of everything. But I brushed it off, it was our turn now.

"So how was your summer?" I asked looking at Jake.

"Very good," he responded, "I took some summer classes, and worked at UPS."

"You still dating Amy?" asked Dave.

Amy Criswell was a fairly attractive girl. Quiet and shy, but she always seemed like such a good girl. Her dad was an evangelist, and was becoming more well known each year. He always seemed like a fairly decent guy.

"Yeah, Amy and I are still together," responded Jake, "So don't you guys get any ideas."

We all laughed. Admittedly, Amy was an attractive girl, and most guys would consider themselves lucky to be able to date a girl like

18

her. But for some reason, there was something about her that put me off. Looking back, I understand why, but I'll get into that later. Tony had started dating a girl at the middle of the last school year, but had broken up with her toward the end of the semester. He had said that she had a rebellious attitude, and we all accepted that. I still don't know what happened to that girl. She never came back to college. But now it was the beginning of a new year. Which meant that all of us would be looking for girlfriends soon. That is the nature of the beast. The previous school year, I had noted that guys who weren't dating, or who weren't actively trying to get a date were labeled as "gay." At least until they started dating.

"Got your eyes on any prospects yet Jason?" asked Tony with a smile and a wink. We all knew that I had a bit of an upper hand on the dating thing. With my dad being a famous preacher, it would be hard not to be able to find a date.

"I've seen a couple of girls I might ask out, but I'm waiting" I responded. I didn't want to get all caught up on this yet. I was hoping to find a good girl, who was looking for a husband who would be in the ministry, and who was the perfect woman for a preacher.

"Well, there's going to be a date night at the end of the week," said Jake, "You should try to find yourself a girl for that at least."

I nodded my head, since my mouth was full of pizza. The river boat ride, of course. How could I forget? We'd done this last year as well. It was a beginning of the year date night, where we'd go on a river boat ride on the Mississippi River. The school would rent the whole river boat for the night, so we didn't have to listen to ungodly music or be subjected to seeing unsaved couples holding hands or kissing. We weren't allowed to hold hands or anything, and the college needed to know who was with the school and who wasn't.

After we were done with the pizza, we decided to head upstairs, and look around and see what was going on. We walked around, looking at all the people chatting. The sounds of laughter and happiness rang through the hallways as people joked and talked about all the exciting things going on. We all walked over to the mailboxes, where we could get our identification cards. We wouldn't be able to get on campus without our ID, or even get our meals. The college needed to know that only students were getting on campus.

As we walked down the hallway, we passed by a young lady, and I almost felt my breath taken away. She was beautiful. She was obviously Latino, with beautiful brown eyes and dark hair that framed her face like a picture. She looked at me briefly, and I caught her face turn pink as she quickly looked away and kept walking quickly down the hall. I stopped for a moment, and watched after her. Dave pulled me back into the real world as I stood there in stunned silence.

"Hey Romeo, we're here."

I turned and looked, and the guys were all laughing. I felt my face turn red, and I just stuck my key into my mailbox and grabbed my ID card.

"What're you guys laughing at?" I asked.

"Hey, you're the one that came to a dead stop to look at some girl" responded Tony with a grin.

"What, I can't admire a pretty girl?"

"Sure you can, just expect to get teased." Responded Dave laughing.

I could see the guys were having a good laugh at my expense. Fine, I thought, let them get it out. We'll all be dating someone in the next few weeks anyway, and I'd get them back.

That night, there was a special devotional sermon preached for all the students. Pastor Hodge, the president of the college, came in and preached at us for a while. It was the same stuff I heard all the time, so I tuned it out and looked around the room. Pastor Hodge was preaching on standards, and on staying the course. I can still remember the words he preached from the pulpit that night, and on so many other nights and sermons.

"A quitter is worthless in the kingdom of God!" He thundered, "If you quit here, you quit God. And God's not going to put up with a quitter. Why just this last year, a young man quit the college. Two months later, he died in a car accident. If you quit what God has planned for you, God just might plan to make sure you quit permanently!"

After the service, there was an altar call. As was expected, several students went forward to get right with God. After singing a few verses of "Just As I Am," we were dismissed for the night, which meant bedtime. We'd have to be up early the next day for morning devotions, breakfast, and classes. I went back to my room, to find out that I was the only upperclassman in my room. Great, I thought to myself, just what I needed. I turned out the lights, to the dismay of my other roommates, but as soon as they started grumbling, I reminded them I outranked them and told them all to shut up. I was tired and cranky. A good night's sleep would cure what ailed me.

Chapter Two:

School Begins

"Rise and shine! Everybody out of bed," Jake said with a booming voice, "get up folks, got a big day today!"   I looked at him and laughed wryly. "You're way too cheerful at 6:30"

He laughed and went on his way down the hall. I grabbed my stuff and walked down to the showers, where all the other sophomores were already. I reached into one of the showers and turned it on.

"Morning guys," I muttered, only half awake, "start of another school year."

"Yep," said Dave, "we'll have to start getting up earlier soon to beat the frogs to the shower. God knows I don't like cold water."

We all laughed. The hot water heaters in the college weren't big enough to keep the water hot for long. I had learned the last year to take quick showers when the water was cold, and didn't want to have to do it again this year. Cold water was for those who didn't get up early enough. Just the thought of it sent a chill down my back. It wasn't a fun experience. After getting showered and shaved, I got dressed and headed up to the chapel for male devotions. As soon as we were all in there, Bro Chapin, the Dean of Men, came out and read a couple Bible verses, then spoke about the importance of doing well in our studies.

After devotions, some of the guys took off for breakfast. I went back down to my room, and grabbed my briefcase, which I had filled with necessary books, pens, and paper. I had a half hour until class started, so I walked up to the Colonial Court. The Colonial Court was like an on-campus restaurant, that served a number of dishes for students. I grabbed a couple candy bars, and then walked over to a table and started eating. As I ate, I flipped through some of the curriculum for my new classes. This semester, I'd be taking Greek, Sophomore English, Music, Biographies of Fundamental Heroes, and Church Methodology. Church Methodology was a standard class taken by male students. We were required to take four years of that class, three if we had an A average. It was the same thing over and over, how to perform a wedding, run a bus route, pick a song leader, and all the other things that had to be done in church. Frankly, it was a boring class. Not many people cared for it, especially as we had to read through the same book every year.

When chapel finally came that day, I decided I would probably enjoy Greek class the most. I wanted to be able to read the Bible in the original Greek, so I figured that this class would give me the tools I needed. The first chapel of the year was predictable. Almost the same sermon as the one we had in the devotion the other night. But most of the preacher boys were back on their feet during most of the preaching, whooping and hollering and shouting "amen." To be honest, I did my share of that too. It was expected of us, though I didn't really understand why. Looking back, I can see that the preachers' encouraged it, because it made them feel like they were doing a good job. When chapel was over that day, they announced that Friday night would be the first date night of the year. I determined then to find the girl that I had seen the day before. I still wasn't able to get her out of my mind.

The next day went almost like any other. Classes were the same, and chapel was the same. As I headed to the cafeteria for lunch, I was stopped dead in my tracks. There she was again, standing in the sunlight near the front doors, laughing with a friend. Her smile was beautiful, joy seemed to radiate from her very being. The sunlight cast a golden glow about her, as if it was a scene from a painting. I suddenly felt a sharp elbow in my ribs, and I turned to see Tony grinning beside me.

"Well bro, you gonna get her name or what?"

"Yeah . . . yeah, I'm gonna go get her name."

"C'mon bro, you got it," said Dave who was now standing beside Tony, "show us what you got."

I laughed nervously, then turned and looked back at her. I caught her gaze for a moment, and she suddenly looked away, seeming bashful, and embarrassed she had been caught looking. That only emboldened me, and I walked over toward her, trying not to let anyone see that I was a nervous wreck inside. Although I didn't know why I was so nervous, after all, she was just a girl. I could have my pick of almost any girl on campus, being the son of a famous preacher. It would be no problem for me to pursue almost any girl there. But this one had me twisting in the wind. I approached her with all the calm and courage I could muster.

"H-Hi, I'm Jason," I said looking at her, searching for the right words to use next. But as I hesitated, she spoke next.

"Hi Jason, I'm Christina."

I looked at her, and blurted out "I'm going on the river boat ride Friday."

She looked at me, slightly amused, and said "Oh?"

"I-I mean, I was w-wondering if you'd like to go on the river boat ride with me." I could feel my face turning twenty shades of red, and felt almost certain that she could see that I was so nervous I was about to fall over from shaking.

She smiled, and looked at me, "I'd love to go with you."

Instantly, I felt relaxed, and once again, I thought myself in charge of the situation. I knew that my next move was to tell her when I would be ready to meet her before the ride.

"Well, the busses leave at 6:30pm, and we can meet in the lobby at 6pm."

"That sounds nice," she said.

I wasn't sure exactly what to say next. I'd never been this tongue-tied around a girl before. And I knew she was a freshman, and I a sophomore, so I should be in charge of the situation. Instead, I felt helpless in her presence, like a little child only now learning to walk. I decided I needed to retreat and regroup.

"Well, I guess I'll see you later on campus, and we'll talk again before Friday," I said looking into her eyes, "I've gotta get to lunch, so I'll see you later."

Her eyes sparkled a little, perhaps dancing with laughter I thought at the time, and she responded, "Of course, I need to meet my friends for lunch too."

And with that, we parted ways for the afternoon. I walked back to Tony and Dave, and walked into the cafeteria together. We got to our table, where Mike and Jake were waiting. I dove straight into my food, as Tony and Dave replayed the entire scene where I asked out Christina with great hilarity. Mike and Jake both laughed heartily at my blurting out "I'm going on the river boat ride!" By the end of lunch, I was laughing along with them.

By the time Friday came around, I'd already met with Christina again. I had learned she was a bus kid from the inner city of Memphis. She lived in a mostly Latino neighborhood, and was a second generation Mexican-American. She was saved when a couple of bus workers came to her house one Saturday afternoon, and when she was a teenager she started going to Memphis Metro Baptist Inner City School.

I stood in the lobby, waiting somewhat anxiously for her to appear. She soon came, and we sat and talked while we waited for the busses to be ready. While we were on our way to the river boat, we spent the entire ride just talking about the four gospels and how they intertwined. At this point, my mind couldn't quite grasp the fact that I was having an intelligent discussion with a woman on something like doctrine. I had always learned that God made men to understand doctrine, and women were supposed to learn from their husband or their father, and never put a word in edgewise about the subject. It felt odd to me to discuss such matters with her, but I also felt that now I had found someone to talk to about things in the Bible who wouldn't just be giving me the pat answers I'd been given all my life. Strangely, this was all reassuring to me.

Back in my bed that night, I thought over the events of the day gone by. It seemed odd to me, that I could have such a deep conversation with a member of the opposite gender. And yet, it felt normal, like it was the way things were supposed to be. After a while, I fell asleep.

Over the course of the next couple weeks, Christina and I were seeing each other on a regular basis. Most of the time, we'd meet each other in the Colonial Court, where we'd have a sundae or a burger. We'd sometimes sit and discuss scripture or have devotions together. I always found it such a change, just reading what the Bible says for itself and talking it over, rather than just listening to what was said in the pulpit.

Classes progressed as normal, some classes were quite dull, while others were lively. Church methodology was boring normally, but occasionally would get exciting whenever one of the preachers felt the preacher boys needed a little preaching at, and he'd get all wound up and let loose. I did all right in my classes, never getting lower than a C grade, and normally an A or B.

One morning, I dropped in at my room between classes. Much to my surprise, I found Jake, Bro Chapin, and Dr. Towler the college vice president in my room. They all seemed startled slightly that I had come in, and they all hesitated at first. Bro Chapin was the first to speak.

"Hi Jason, what do you need?"

"I came down to grab a notepad," I responded. I could see Jake was going through Adam's trunk. But I didn't ask any questions. I knew better than to ask questions. They suspected somebody in my room of something, but I didn't know what yet.

"Jason, do you know of any unapproved reading material in the room here?" Dr. Towler asked.

"No sir, I haven't seen anything."

"Well, it seems your roommate Adam had a copy of Sports Illustrated in here. He's going to be shipped by the end of the day."

I nodded my head soberly. I'd seen guys get kicked out before because of something like that, but never in my own room. This was something new entirely for me. I grimly thought of the times I'd listened to Adam talk of the Bible and God. Had it all just been a ploy on his part to keep us distracted? I'd never know, because I didn't see Adam again. During the chapel sermon that day, Dr. Towler had gotten up and had preached on the evils of Sports Illustrated, Playboy, and just about every other magazine under the sun. Half of the sermon was addressed to the ladies, telling them if they didn't dress right, they would be forcing the preacher boys to lust after them, and in God's eyes, they would be nothing more than prostitutes. He likened them to the harlot in Proverbs, the one who led the simple astray. The preacher boys in the "Amen Corner" ate this up, by the end of the service, Dr. Towler had them in a frenzy, they were standing on the pews shouting

28

and yelling. And then he dropped the hammer. He announced a student would be leaving that day who had been caught with a magazine. One could hear a collective gasp roll across the auditorium, students looked back and forth at each other, everybody was wondering who it could be. I saw Adam sitting down front, near Bro Chapin. I felt sorry for him, knowing that everybody would be talking about him for days to come. But he shouldn't have done it, I rationalized to myself. He's brought this whole thing on himself. Now God can't use him anymore, and it's all because of those whores in those magazines.

Then the invitation came. Dr Towler called for everybody to repent of their sin. He called on all the young ladies to repent of any sin they may have committed that could have caused a preacher boy to stumble. People were practically tripping over themselves to get to the front. I knelt by my pew, knowing full well that if I didn't, I could be singled out for being rebellious.

That night, I walked back to my room, and looked at the empty bed near the door. I almost felt a pang of guilt for forcing him toward that bunk. I say almost, because I didn't really feel much of anything over the matter. He made his bed I thought, now let him lie in it. He knows what God expects of him, and he shouldn't have done what he did. As I got ready for bed, I saw Kyle walk in the room. He stopped and looked at the empty bed, and I immediately felt sorry for him. Kyle and Adam had been really close, and I could see the sadness in his eyes. As he started getting ready for bed, the door was pushed open by a couple of freshmen preacher boys from down the hall.

"Hey Kyle," one said with glee, "Where's your buddy Adam?"

"Yeah Kyle, ain't your buddy around anymore?" asked the other.

"Hey guys, get out of here" I ordered.

"What? You're telling us what to do?"

"Yes, now get out. This isn't your room."

I walked over and slammed the door shut in their faces. I turned and looked at Kyle, just in time to see him wipe away a tear. I pretended I didn't see that action. I walked back over to my bed.

"For what it's worth Kyle," I said, "I'm sorry about Adam."

Kyle nodded his head, but said nothing. That day, something changed inside of him, it was like he had been broken. His best friend was gone, and little had I known that Adam was his only friend. Adam and Kyle had grown up next door to each other, and it had been Adam who invited Kyle to church for the first time, and who had persuaded him to come to Bible college instead of the local university that had offered him a full scholarship. The teasing got worse, and Kyle encountered it everywhere. The guys wouldn't leave him alone about it when he was by himself. Since he and I were roommates, I felt a duty to protect him when we were together, but mostly I stayed out of the situation. One day I walked down to my dorm floor. I heard yelling as I got to the bottom of the stairs, and I hurried to get to my room.

"Take it back!" I heard Kyle yell. I knew right away something was wrong. Kyle never raised his voice.

"I said, Adam is a dirty fag, and that's why he got kicked out of college!" One of the other freshmen was yelling right back at Kyle. By the time I had gotten there, there was a crowd gathered around my door. All of the sudden, I saw a body fly through the door, Kyle had pushed him out. The other guy hit the wall, and looked at Kyle in surprise. Kyle came running out of the room, and I saw him pull his fist back and land a heavy punch on the boy's head. Nobody moved at first, it was like it was happening in slow motion. Then Kyle began to land more punches, and blood began to flow from the other boy's face. I knew I had to stop the fight, and I pushed my way through the crowd, yelling at Kyle to stop. I saw somebody take off running to get security, and I knew I had to end this fast. But Kyle just pushed me back, and continued his beating.

"Tony, Dave, give me a hand here guys!" I yelled as I grabbed one of Kyle's arms. Tony and Dave were pushing their way through the crowd, and they helped me pull Kyle back into the room.

"Get that kid out of here," I yelled to the others standing around. I turned and looked at Kyle, who by this time had begun to calm down. Then, he looked at his fist and saw the blood. Dave, Tony, and I all looked at each other. Then Kyle started crying. He grabbed a towel and started wiping off the blood as he kept crying, open and unashamed.

"Why couldn't people just leave it alone?" he asked.

I knew I didn't have an answer for him. I just sat beside him for a moment. Then Kyle got up, and grabbed his suitcase. Tony spoke up first, "What are you doing Kyle?"

"I'm leaving this place," he said, "I guess I was wrong about this college being a good place to learn more about God."

We all stood in stunned silence, scarcely daring to believe he had spoken those words. Kyle packed with amazing efficiency. By the time security got there, he had everything packed and ready to go. And go he did. He grabbed his bags, and pushed past the guards. We followed him out, watching him. Kyle hadn't brought much with him, so he didn't need any help out with his things. Tony, Dave and I followed him to the parking lot, where he loaded his car. He opened his door, and I walked forward.

"Kyle," I said, "I'm sorry."

"Save it for someone who cares," he said coldly, "you can't make yourself feel better with words now."

With that, Kyle jumped in his car and took off. Nobody ever heard from Kyle again, and the kid he beat up also left college shortly after. It left the college in a somber mood for a couple of days, nobody knew really what to do or say. Kyle had been the happy, go-lucky kind of guy. But something had pushed him to the point where he snapped. And it saddened people to see it happen. Christine and I talked about it, and I knew that it would leave an impact on my life, probably forever.

Chapter Three:

Damnable Heresies

After the tragedy of Kyle, things seemed to quiet down for a while. School was back to normal, every so often somebody was leaving, but that was the nature of college. Some folks were cut out for it, and some weren't. Christine and I were still dating, and I knew I was falling for her, hard and fast. Besides her stunning good looks, I was struck by her obvious intelligence. And there was something else about her as well. Something many of the other girls were lacking. I couldn't exactly describe it, but she just seemed to be the definition of a godly woman. She wasn't at all what I had been looking for, in fact, she was more.

One day, I was talking with Tom, another student. We got on the topic of Romans 8 and predestination. I made a couple remarks that he took a great umbrage to, probably because they were Calvinistic comments. The next day, I found a note from Dr. Towler in my mailbox, wanting a counseling session with me that afternoon. When I got to his office, he asked me to have a seat.

"Jason, I wanted to bring you in here to talk to you about something."

"Yes sir, what about?"

"Well, I wanted to ask you a question."

"What's that sir?"

"Are you a Calvinist," he asked, eyes slightly narrowing.

"I think so," I responded hesitantly, "but I'm not really sure."

"Well son, I need to talk to you about that. What kind of Calvinist are you?"

"Sir?" I asked, puzzled by his question.

"Are you a Lapsarianist, or a Supralapsarianist?"

"I don't know what those terms mean sir," I responded, genuinely puzzled by his question. He looked at me, obviously exasperated. "Well son, you're the Calvinist, I'm just asking you what you believe about your own theology!"

"Well, to be honest with you sir, I don't know much about the subject, I guess you could say I believe in all five points."

"Why?" he asked.

"Well, I guess they just make sense to me sir."

We then had a half-hour conversation where he lectured me on the evils of Calvinism, never once permitting me the chance to bring any Scripture for my defense. The conversation went everywhere, from how I must be a lazy soulwinner because I was a Calvinist, to how I don't know what my theology is, so I don't really know what I'm talking about.

"Son, didn't you just get saved last year?" he asked.

"Yes sir, but . . . "

He cut me off, "And you presume to tell me, somebody who's been saved much longer, that I'm wrong about the Bible?"

I didn't answer him. I couldn't answer him. I knew that in

reality, there was no answer that he would accept. But he took my silence as submission, and he showed me the door.   That day in chapel, Pastor Hodge got up to preach, and he spent the entire chapel service preaching against the evils of Calvinism. I knew that the sermon was intended for me, and being able to preach it in the chapel was just another way of warning the students of the dangers of such an evil doctrine. I felt embarrassed, even though I knew that almost nobody there knew who was being preached about. It was a warning, nothing more. Despite who my father was, I knew I had just gotten a warning. I decided it would be best for me to stay silent on the matter.

Later at lunch, I spoke quietly with Christina about the subject. Christina was upset, and horrified that I had been talked to in such a manner.

"He really said that to you?" she asked keeping her voice low.

"Yes," I responded, "but it doesn't really bother me. I'm not going to worry about it."

She looked at me, her soft brown eyes seemed unusually saddened by this. I brushed it off as just typical female worrying. My mom did that a lot. But the concern in Christina's voice was evident.

"Don't worry Christina. I'll handle it."

She just nodded her head. Something was troubling her, but I didn't ask her what. Something told me to just let it go. Christina had work in the afternoon, and I tried to cheer her up before work. When it was time for her to go, she left in a bit of a better mood, although still worried about me. I went back to my schoolwork. My work during the summer had my tuition already paid for, so I didn't need to get a job out at school. And my mom would send care packages for me, and my dad would slip in a little cash for extras.

As I was walking back to my room, I heard my name being called. I turned around to look, and to my surprise it was Pastor Hodge.

"Jason, would you mind taking a walk with me?"

"No, not at all sir," I said.

We stepped out of the building. It was bright outside, and a little cool. We walked in the direction of the athletic field. I had met Pastor Hodge on numerous occasions, he could be a nice man, but against enemies he was a fierce combatant. We walked in silence for a few moments, and then he spoke.

"Jason, what exactly do you know about Calvinism?"

"Well sir, I guess I just really know the five main points."

"Son, do you understand that this damnable heresy has caught up many in its lie, and has killed many a church? You could ruin your father's ministry if you were to start telling people you were a Calvinist."

I thought for a moment. I knew well what Pastor Hodge was looking for. He wanted me to admit defeat, and give up the notion of Calvinism. And I knew what not doing so meant. I would be targeted by staff and faculty. My dad would probably be called. Everything I did would be under scrutiny.

"To be honest Pastor Hodge, what Dr. Towler said today made a lot of sense to me."

"What do you mean?" he asked, his voice sounding almost triumphant as if he knew the answer already.

36

"Well sir, it's like you said today in chapel, Calvinists make lousy soulwinners. How can I be both at the same time?"

"I'm glad you're starting to see the truth son. For a couple weeks though, I want you to continue your counseling sessions with Dr. Towler."

"Yes sir," I said, "I'll do that."

With that, our informal meeting was over. I walked back into the college, feeling low, knowing that I had just prostituted myself in order to keep myself looking good to Pastor Hodge. I knew that I had no pride left. This was something that I had always thought was beyond me, selling out my convictions in order to maintain my status. But I had, and now I had to bear this. And I couldn't dare tell Christina. What would she say if she knew I had sold my soul? The guilt I carried now was mine alone.

I walked back to my room, feeling dejected. I sat in my room, wondering how I could ever face Christina again. I picked up my Bible, and began to read the Psalms. Slowly, I could feel peace coming over me. I lay down to take a nap, and as I took my nap, I began to dream. As I dreamed, I found myself standing in the college alone. I looked down the hallway, and saw a figure walking towards me. Then I heard a voice speaking to me.

"Jason, don't be discouraged. Your time has not yet come. Know that I love you, and will always be there for you."

I suddenly awoke, half expecting to see someone in my room. I realized it had all been a dream, a pleasant dream, given the day I had. I felt like I just had heard a message from God. Something stirred inside me now. I knew that there was something more to this, I would have to be patient and wait on God now.

I walked back up to Colonial Court, and decided to wait for Christina to get off work. I studied for an upcoming test, while eating a burger. Christina got off, and joined me for a sundae.

"So how's the rest of your day gone?" she asked.

"Everything is going to be all right," I said confidently, "I know God's still got something special for me eventually."

She smiled, "I know that already."

I looked at her, rather puzzled. And she stood up, "I've gotta go to my room and study, but I"ll see you tomorrow. I'll be praying for you." And with that, she got up and walked back to her room. I allowed myself a moment to watch her walk away.

Calvinism wasn't welcome at TBBC. I had to learn that the hard way, but at least I got off easier than most students would. But it was only because of who my father was. I heard later that another student had been discovered with several of Spurgeon's sermons in his possession, and he was made an example to others of what happens to Calvinists. He was campused for the rest of the semester. I felt sorry for him, and I realized it was my fault that he was made into a scapegoat for this.

Chapter Four:

Walking in the Rain

There's a hundred different reasons to start dating at Bible college, especially TBBC. For one thing, you're more likely to find a committed Christian. But if you don't date, it's highly likely that you'll be accused of being a queer. Sorry, I mean gay. But gay doesn't get used much at TBBC, you're more likely to hear queer. We're not allowed to say "fag" so some preachers use "Six Flags" in reference to gays. I'm not sure why exactly, but that's what happens.

Christina is the first girl I've been in a serious relationship with. Well, maybe I shouldn't call her a girl. She's a lady, a woman. Classy in her own way, and so much more mature than any of the other girls around here. She's not looking for someone who's on his way up the IFB ladder. She's looking for someone who loves Christ, and who will love her. That's one of the qualities that has caused me to fall for her. She's not just a "yes girl" like so many of the others around here, who are so desperate for a husband, that they are afraid to disagree with any guy they date. We've disagreed some, but never really fought. It's not like we've argued over anything huge, but sometimes we see things a little differently. We both have a lot of the same goals, we just see different ways to achieve them.

I suppose it important to mention that Christina and I had a long talk the other day. She cried as she told me some things, but surprisingly, none of those things mattered to me like I thought they would. As I looked into her soft brown eyes that were filling up with tears, I just wanted to take her in my arms and tell her that everything was okay now. I wanted to tell her I'd never let her go, and she was safe with me. It hurt so much that I couldn't just hold her and let her know that I'd always be her protector. But like it or not, those are the rules at TBBC. You can barely even shake a woman's hand on campus, without getting in trouble. And forget helping a woman up if she slips and falls,

40

it might cause you to lust through touching her.

A couple of days after this, Dr. McKinzie was preaching in chapel, on relationships and dating. I don't suppose one could call that preaching at all, more of a relationship advice seminar. I listened to him drone on for some time, all about the proper methods of dating, and what young ladies must do to attract a man.

"Girls, you need to know, that the way you dress directly affects your boyfriend. Always take the utmost care to dress modestly so you don't cause him to lust after you. It's only normal that a guy lusts, but if you're not dressed properly, it's like putting a ham hock in front of a rottweiler with a cage between the two. That dog is gonna sit there and salivate for hours and the sight and thought of that ham hock. Be careful in how you dress."

"Guys, you need to be one hundred percent in control of the date. You need to be the one to plan the date. Plan every activity, plan what you two will talk about, make sure you follow the outline of your date so you don't get caught up talking about something inappropriate. Many a young man has been led astray by a woman because he didn't plan their dates properly. And girls, know that a guy will always go as far as you let him. So it's up to you ladies, to set the standard for the relationship. You hold the key not only to your purity, but also to your boyfriend's purity. You control how far he goes, don't let him cross the line."

"And girls, remember, when you're doing activities on your date that you never beat your boyfriend at a game. Shame, shame I say, on any young lady who shows up her boyfriend by beating him in a

41

*game, especially if it's a physical activity like miniature golf or
bowling. Even if you're better, you let him win. Shame on any woman
who doesn't build up her man by letting him win."*

For the first time, I was really disturbed by this teaching on
dating. It didn't seem logical, to place all these burdens on women,
when men can obviously control themselves.

"What kind of egocentric man needs his woman to allow him
to win in order that he feel good about himself?"

I thought to myself about my relationship with Christina. We
didn't follow these guidelines on our dates, or for ourselves as a couple.
And yet, our relationship was so great. She clearly allowed me to take
the lead, but it was because she respected me and not because she felt
she had to. I didn't want to overpower Christina's personality, and I
certainly didn't want to quench her abilities. The chapel service
troubled me, something wasn't right about it.

After chapel, I went out to my mailbox to check for any mail.
As was becoming usual, there was a note from Christina in my box. I
smiled to myself, and placed it in my back pocket. The other envelope
was from Dr Towler. I opened it, curious as to what he wanted. The
note was a request to see me after lunch in his office.

When I got to Dr Towler's office, Pastor Hodge was there too.
They asked me to have a seat, and I sat down in a chair facing both of
them. Pastor Hodge spoke first.

"Jason, I understand that you are dating Christina Lopez."

"Yes sir, that's right."

Dr Towler spoke "So, how is that going?"

42

"It's going well sir, I really like Christina."

There was a pause, and they looked at each other. "Well Jason, I'm a little sorry to hear that," said Pastor Hodge.

"I'm sorry sir?" I answered puzzled as to his response.

"Well Jason, it's just that we don't feel that Christina is a good match for you."

"Why is that sir? Christina and I get along great."

"Well son," said Dr Towler, "Christina...well, she's not the type of girl for an up and coming preacher boy like yourself."

"You see Jason, a young man like yourself needs a woman who is going to complement you, someone who is a fitting ornament for someone who is going places." said Pastor Hodge.

"I'm sorry sir, I really don't understand what you're getting at here," I responded, "what exactly is wrong with Christina?"

"Well, Jason, surely you've noticed that you and Christina come from two totally separate backgrounds. And I'm not certain that she is a good influence on you. You need someone who will be a good influence on you as a Christian."

"I don't really understand, we are both Christians."

Dr Towler spoke, "Jason, you're the son of a well known preacher. Christina is the daughter of a drunk, who doesn't even know who her father is. I mean, doesn't that tell you that you and her are totally different people?"

My face turned red, but this time because I was angry. "Christina isn't her parents. She's a Christian who loves the Lord, how can you say that she isn't fit for me just because of who her parents are?

So what if she grew up on the wrong side of town?"

"Calm down Jason, just hear us out."

"You see Jason, a young man like yourself should be dating a young lady who is the daughter of someone in full-time ministry. Somebody who will understand the struggles of the ministry, and who will understand that a preacher can't always be home. Can you really say that Christina understands this? Can you really say that she'll be the type of woman who works beside you to make the most of your ministry?" asked Pastor Hodge.

"Jason, you're not thinking clearly right now. You've been dating this girl for too long. I mean, think about all the implications of this relationship. She's a bus kid, her parents aren't Christians. You were raised in a Christian family. The bus kids are important to God yes, but they can lead a good church kid astray. You're white, and the son of a preacher. She's Mexican, and doesn't know her father. You come from two totally separate cultures. Sure, you may think you love her, but what about in five years when the two of you are fighting over things that could have been avoided if you'd dated someone from your own background?" said Dr Towler.

By now I was angrier than I'd ever been. I looked at Dr Towler and said "So what you're saying is because I'm white and she's not, our relationship isn't going to work?"

"Now hold on Jason, I didn't say that."

"No, but that's what you meant, isn't it? I mean, here I am, the white son of a famous white preacher, and you don't want me dating a Latino girl. Why can others here date Latinos', and it not be a problem for them?"

"Now Jason, don't think this is just about Latino and white..." started Pastor Hodge.

"No sir, I'm well aware it's not solely about that, I'm aware that you think the son of a famous preacher shouldn't date a Latino, because you're afraid of how it'll make you look."

They both stopped dead in their tracks and looked at each other. I wasn't taking this as well as they'd hoped.

Pastor Hodge spoke, "Jason, as your pastor here at college, I'm telling you, not to see her anymore."

I stopped and looked at him. My mind was racing now, in IFB culture, if the pastor says it, it may as well be law. You have to do what the pastor says, otherwise you're outside of the will of God, and God's not going to protect you. I knew that if I refused him, I would be marked at the college. My dad would be called, and I would be ripped up and down by him. It was likely that I would also be placed on restriction as well, and all the staff and faculty would be watching me. I knew I loved Christina, but I also knew that my life as I knew it would be over if I chose her. That is, if I was even allowed to speak to her again before they campused me. I sat there quietly, as the two of them spoke to me some more, listing the dangers I would be in if I chose to continue my relationship with Christina. "God has put us over you for a reason, you need to listen" they told me. I felt a tear welling up, but I played it off and quickly wiped it away. I knew I could show no sign of weakness.

When they finished speaking, I got up from my chair to leave.

They both stood up with me, and walked me to the office door. Pastor Hodge gripped my hand firmly, and looked me in the eye.

"Remember Jason, we're going to be watching you. Be careful who you allow on you, that they are good influences. Don't worry, we'll find you a good girl."

I had a feeling I knew who that good girl would be. Dr Towler's daughter was my own age, and while attractive, lacked any personality. I knew I didn't want to date someone like her. I needed something more.

I didn't see Christina after work that night, when she got back, she went straight to her room to study for a test in the morning. After spending some time pretending to study, I walked back to my dorm room, and got in bed. I lay there for several hours, staring up at the bunk above me, thinking. I thought of Christina, and the warmth of her smile. I knew I loved her, and that I couldn't give her up. No matter what the others said. I decided that I would make this clear tomorrow. Turned out, they weren't going to give me a chance.

Chapter Five:

Through Christina's Eyes

Jason and I were progressing well in our relationship. I could tell he was falling for me, and I was falling for him. I decided there were some things about myself I needed to tell him. After all, our relationship needed to be based on honesty and trust. And I trusted him with my heart.

I looked across the table at Jason. His piercing blue eyes danced with laughter as he told a funny story from his bus route the previous week. His dark hair seemed such a contrast to his fair skin and blue eyes. He always spoke with such passion and conviction when we talked of serious issues. It was easy to see that he had the potential to be a gifted preacher. When it came to spiritual things, he spoke with a command that I didn't see in the other preacher boys. Rather than bluster his way through something with talking points learned from others, he backed up his convictions with scripture.

Finally, I looked at him, and knew now was the moment to talk to him. I didn't really want to talk about it, but I had to.

"Jason, could we go for a walk outside?"

"Sure, it's a nice day for a walk."

We stepped out into the warm sunlight. A cool breeze blew across the campus, it was a welcome change from the heat of summer. I always loved the fall, with the summer drawing to a close, and the winter coming, fall was like a clash of seasons where the old summer and young winter wrestled for control. Jason and I walked over towards the football field.

"Jason, I need to talk to you about something."

Jason looked at me, his eyes had turned serious as he heard the tone of my voice. "Okay, what do you need to talk about?"

"Let's sit down on the stands."

We sat down, he sat next to me, and turned to face me so he could give me his undivided attention. I turned away from his gaze for a moment, then sighed as I steeled myself for the conversation that was coming.

"Jason, I want to talk to you about some things in my past."

He looked at me in surprise, "You know, I don't need to hear all about what you did when you were younger Christina."

"I know you feel that way Jason, and I'm glad, I really am. But I feel like I need to talk to you about it, so if you could just hear me out please."

Jason nodded soberly. He could tell this was troubling me, and now his eyes were troubled. He looked at me, waiting for me to speak. And finally, I did.

"Jason, I-I was molested when I was younger. My mother dated a guy for a while, who sometimes would end up in my bedroom. I guess I was about ten or eleven when it started, but my mom broke up with him fairly quickly, so it didn't last for that long. But it was more than long enough. I remember closing my eyes and praying that he would go away. I could hear his heavy breathing when he came down the hall at night, and I would wish I was anywhere but there. When he came in my room, I just stared at the ceiling and pretended I was somewhere else. When I got older, and started going to high school, I was dating a senior as a freshman. Well, maybe not dating. I-It was more of being a partner with him. I thought I was dating him, but it turns out, he was just using me when he and his girlfriend were on the outs. We slept together several times, until I heard him laughing to his buddies about how he had put one over on me. Jason, all I ever wanted was to be loved. I never knew my father, and so whenever any guy showed interest in me, I relished that attention. It made me feel special, like for one magical moment, all the world was right. When I got saved,

I was still thinking like that. At least for a while. When I started going to Metro's schools, Dan Harris showed a lot of interest in me, and he and I dated for a while. Until security caught us on campus once, and he and I both were lectured by Pastor Hodge. I was almost kicked out, until I thought I might be pregnant, then they just shushed everything up. I haven't been the perfect girl Jason, and I don't know how I can be worthy of you with the type of life I've lived. That's why I've been so scared of getting seriously close to you. I've been afraid that maybe you wouldn't love me if you knew what was in my past. I know I don't deserve it, but I want your forgiveness Jason."

I took a deep breath and swallowed. I could feel tears flowing down my cheeks, and Jason handed me his handkerchief. I looked at his eyes, which no longer were laughing, but were now sad. I wished I could read what was going on in his mind, what thoughts he now had about me.

"Surely he must think I'm used merchandise, that I'm no longer worthy of him" I told myself bitterly. For too long, I'd held in these secrets. I just wanted to know that someone, someday would make everything alright for me again. I looked back at him, and his eyes locked onto mine as he started to speak.

"Christina, you're obviously a different person than you were those years ago. It doesn't matter to me what you did in your past, it matters to me who you are now. We aren't living in the past. Christina, no matter what you did in your past, it's not enough to make me stop loving you."

I stopped crying. Had I really heard what I thought I heard?

50

Had he just said that he loved me? I was certain I had heard it, but I couldn't be sure. I looked back up into his eyes, and I could see it then. He really did. He said he loved me, and from his eyes, I could see he meant what he said. And for one shining moment, the entire world stopped and everything faded away. All I could see was him. I wished I could reach out and cry on his shoulder, and was tempted to do so in spite of the rules.

I wiped the tears from my eyes, and smiled. "Well, I guess we better go back inside."

He smiled and looked at me, "Yeah, I guess. Let's go."

The entire way back, he laughed and joked with me, until I forgot I had been crying just a few moments before. The sun was back in my life, and I just knew it was there to stay.

The next morning, Dr Towler's secretary came up to pull me out of my first period class. I was surprised and confused. I didn't understand why Dr Towler wanted to see me. When I got to his office, he wasn't the only one seated there. Pastor Hodge was as well.

"Christina, we need to have a chat with you," said Dr Towler.

"Christina, I'd like to talk to you about Jason," said Pastor Hodge.

I looked at him in surprise, it didn't make sense. Why did they want to talk to me about Jason. Was there something I needed to know?

"Christina, we're concerned that you and Jason don't make a good match. I understand that the two of you have feelings for each other, but you're two totally different people."

"Pastor Hodge, Jason and I aren't totally different. We may

have two different backgrounds, but we understand each other perfectly."

"I'm glad you see my point Christina, it's your backgrounds that I'm concerned about."

"I don't understand what you mean."

Dr Towler spoke "Christina, what would Jason say if he knew that you had been with another young man from this college only a couple short years ago?"

I felt my blood chill, "What are you saying?"

"Do you think Jason would be so eager to date you if he found out you were used merchandise? We had a talk with Jason yesterday about you."

My heart plummeted, what had they said to him? My mind raced in a hundred different directions. I felt a lump in my throat.

"Christina, as of this morning, you are campused. You are not permitted to speak to Jason at all for now. You're only allowed to leave campus for work or for church and Christian service."

Pastor Hodge stood up, "Christina, we are going to be watching you. If you insist on speaking to Jason, you will be in more trouble."

I looked at the two of them, more confused than ever. I hadn't broken any rules, and now they were campusing me? Something didn't seem right to me, but I knew better than to argue. Surely Jason hadn't raised my hopes yesterday just to dash them against the ground this morning.

As soon as I left Dr Towler's office, I went straight to my

room. I needed a good cry, and cry I did. I couldn't believe that this was happening to me. Just as I felt like God was putting everything on track, it seemed like he pulled the carpet out from under me.

When chapel came, I did as I was told, and avoided Jason. But I didn't see Jason anywhere to avoid him. I looked across the chapel to see if I could find him, but he wasn't sitting in our regular spot. I felt a lump in my throat, and quickly swallowed it. I was determined not to let them see me cry.

I went the rest of the day without seeing Jason. After chapel, he was nowhere to be found. Even though I couldn't talk to him, I wanted just to see him, and look in his eyes and see what they told me. I was angry that I didn't see him in the lunchroom. And angrier still that he was nowhere tot be found after lunch.

I walked back to my room to get ready for work. When I got there, I found an envelope on my pillow. My roommate Julie looked at me, and explained.

"Jason asked me to give this to you. He told me to keep it quiet, and I told him I would. I didn't read it or anything."

I grabbed it and stuffed it in my purse. I'd read it later while I was at work. Jason had found a way to communicate with me, that was all I needed to know.

Chapter Six:

Jason's Problem

I didn't sit in our normal place in chapel the next day. I sat in the back of the chapel, where I could see Christina anxiously looking for me. The sadness and worried expression on her face was apparent to me. I was angry, frustrated that the administration would do something like this to us. I didn't pay much attention in chapel that day, and instead focused on writing a note that I would have given to her by her roommate.

Dear Christina,

By now you probably know that the college administration doesn't want us together. I'm fairly certain I know the exact reason why, but I don't want to say yet. Do know however, that I'm not giving up on us. I fully intend that we stay together, regardless of the cost. You are the only one I love, and I hope you understand that. Keep an eye out for more messages until I figure out what we should do.

All My Love,

Jason

I found Julie after chapel, and asked her to give the note to Christina, and to keep it quiet. Julie nodded her head and accepted. She was a sophomore, and she and I had been good friends the previous year, and I knew that she'd help me. She had no real reason to follow the administration blindly.

After lunch, Tony and I sat in the Colonial Court studying for an upcoming test. After a few moments, I looked at him and decided to talk with him about what was going on.

"Hey Tony, let me ask you about something."

"Sure Jason, what's up?"

"What would you do if the administration told you to stop dating Alyssa?"

Tony's brow furrowed, "What do you mean?"

I explained the whole story to him. I could see the shock registered in his eyes, this was unheard of. The college might forbid a couple from seeing each other if one was genuinely a troublemaker, or if they were getting too hot and heavy. But not simply because of background.

Tony sighed and looked at me, "I guess you have to do what they say. After all, Pastor Hodge is God's authority in our lives."

I sat silent for a moment, "But wouldn't God let me know if there was a problem?

Tony shrugged his shoulders, "I don't know. But I do know if you rebel against the administration, you're going to be in a lot of trouble. You don't want to step outside of the umbrella of protection God placed over you."

We sat on in silence, studying. I thought more about Christina, and the puzzling comments of Pastor Hodge and Dr Towler. When Christina got off work, she normally came into the Colonial Court for a snack, so I sat and waited to catch a glimpse of her again. After what seemed an eternity, the girls came in from work. Christina came in, and glanced at me before she walked by my table, then looked straight ahead and continued by me. As she passed by close to my table, a folded up piece of paper dropped by my feet. I placed my shoe over it, and decided to wait a few moments to pick it up.

Dear Jason,

You have no idea the relief I felt when I read your note. I'm so incredibly frustrated right now, that the college would do this to us. It's not fair! I thought we would be treated like adults here, instead, we're looked at as children incapable of making our own decisions without Pastor Hodge's guidance. I love you too Jason, and I hope you know that I too will not give you up without a fight. I'll be praying, that the two of us can find a way out of this mess, and that God will be the one to show us the way. Let God be your guide in this Jason, don't let the ignorant comments of others push you into making a rash, angry decision.

Love you,

Christina

After reading Christina's note, I began to pray and plot. There had to be a way for the two of us to stay together. We couldn't get married just then, although I suppose if I wanted, we could hop into my car and drive over to Arkansas for a wedding. But that wasn't the way I wanted to do our wedding.

Christina was important to me. I hoped and prayed she knew that. Somehow, someway, I would find an answer to this. I fell asleep that night trying to discover a solution.

Chapter Seven:

Get Right, Be Right

I sat down opposite the chapel from Christina. We could see each other, but not close enough. Chapel that day was going to be preached by Pastor Hodge. Which meant, as is normal, that everybody was taping posters and letters to the pulpit. Whenever Pastor Hodge preached, people would put notes up on the pulpit for him to give them a chapel date with somebody in the chapel. Or trying to set their friends up with somebody. And he would read through a few names, and try to set people up. The guy never had a choice in the matter, but the girl did. So if the girl turned you down, you'd look like a total loser. But normally the girl would say yes, sometimes out of duty or pity, but most of the time just to get a date.

It was always the posters with candy on them that got his attention first. It was funny sometimes, to see the pairings. Jake got set up with Amber Harshberger, a junior from Texas. After a few names were read, I heard my name called. I was a little puzzled, but stood anyway.

"Amanda Harrison, where are you seated?" asked Pastor Hodge.

A hand went up in the air, and Pastor Hodge asked "Would

you like Jason to sit with you in chapel today?"

The answer came back affirmative, although I couldn't hear it myself. I caught Christina's eye as I grabbed my things, and I could tell she wasn't happy. But neither was I. I faked a smile, and sat next to Amanda. She had straight brown hair, but was the daughter of one of the school's vice presidents. I supposed to myself that she was part of the reason they were trying to break me up with Christina. They wanted to pair me with her.

After a couple more names were read, Pastor Hodge began with the days message. He launched into a diatribe about how the pastor was the authority, and how disobeying the pastor would put one out of the will of God. I'd seen him preach this way before, and it meant he was preaching more at somebody, than to us.

"Bless God young people, the pastor is your authority in life, and don't you forget it! If you don't obey your pastor, God's not going to bless you. You need to get right with God if you're not obeying your pastor. He's your God-given authority, and to disobey him is to disobey God. If you're not obeying the authority here at the college, you're not obeying God. If you have problems with the authority here at college, you need to get right with God, and not tell everybody else in the world about it! Students, you need to get right, be right!

Brothers and sisters, young people, we have a traitor in our midst! We have someone here who is working against us, and against God. He has a problem with this school, he has a problem with the authority here."

I started feeling uncomfortable at this point. Was he about to single me out for a tongue lashing from the pulpit? I didn't think he knew about my notes with Christina, or my plans to continue the relationship. And I didn't think he knew about my talk with Tony. Tony wouldn't squeal on me like that.

"Young people, we have someone here who is taking their problems to places where they have no business taking them. That's right, they're spreading gossip and slander about the college, the students, and the administration. There's an internet website, called the Baptist Bralwers Message Board, where they talk about this college, and one of our students is on there posting about this college."

I felt my blood run cold. I had posted on the BBB before I left for college, and I lurked there now while I was at college and private messaged a couple posters there every now and then, but I didn't think I had posted anything about the college. But I hadn't been on there recently. Who was he talking about?

"Let me read you what this young man has written: 'I attend TBBC, and I am constantly appalled at the lack of Godly leadership on campus. I am looking at attending a better Christian College next semester, one where they aren't so legalistic and snooping into the private lives of their own students. A place where you don't get called a queer if you're not actively dating, and where you don't get treated like a second class Christian because your dad isn't in the ministry. TBBC is a joke, and the professors there have no clue what they're talking about half the time. But they expect you to believe whatever they say, and whatever Pastor Hodge says, simply because he's the so-called man of God. Well, let me tell you something I think about this man of God, and that is that nobody can call themselves a man of God if they say the kind of things from the pulpit he says."

I turned and looked back at Dave, and I could see his face was white. He was seated just a couple seats behind me, and he looked at me in the eye. I knew right away it was him. But rather than be angry at him like the others around me, I felt sorry for him. Because I knew what was about to happen. Then I heard Pastor Hodge yell out again.

"Dave Snow stand up!"

Dave stood up silently, and looked Pastor Hodge dead in the eye. I looked at him in awe, not understanding how he could be so calm and have so much courage to stare down Pastor Hodge like that. It amazed me, that he could just stand there like he was.

"Dave Snow, are you the author of this trash?" asked Pastor Hodge.

"It's not trash sir, but yes, I am the author." respond Dave calmly, without raising his voice to yell.

"Well, if you don't like it here so much, why are you here?"

"Sir, I have plans to leave at the end of the semester and attend elsewhere."

"Well son, your plans have changed, because you're leaving now. Security is waiting for you in the back of the auditorium, walk out right now, pack your things, and be gone by lunch."

The guys in the crowd were worked up into a frenzy. Insults were being thrown at him, but Dave calmly left his seat, and started for the back.

"Hey queer, why don't you get saved," someone yelled.

The crowd cheered for that comment, and more students started yelling. Some threats were thrown his way, and somebody tripped him as he got close to the end. A couple guys started throwing punches as he went down, and security had to run and pull him out and escort him the rest of the way out of the auditorium.

Dave stopped and turned before he walked out, and looked over the crowd. He caught my eye, and seemed to try to tell me something before he left. I knew it would be a long time before we could talk again. And I felt something in me tell me to run after him and tell him goodbye, and thank him for being a friend. I felt myself start to move towards the end of the aisle, but I heard to voice of Pastor Hodge again.

"Alright everybody, settle down and have a seat. Let's all sit down and settle down. Young people, look up here."

I sat back down, and looked up. Pastor Hodge spoke a bit, and added a few words about needing to pray for Dave, and then he gave an invitation. Not many people stayed in their seats. Invitation was a show at chapel time, it was a place for everybody to show off how spiritual they were, and how much they were for what the college was for. And nobody was going to miss an opportunity to align themselves with Pastor Hodge and the college this service.

But for once, I stayed in my seat. I just sat down in my seat, and put my head down so nobody could see me shed a tear for Dave. He had been a good friend, and we'd had devotions together more than once. I tried to tell myself he'd opened himself up for this, by posting this on a public message board, but I knew it wasn't true. He didn't deserve to be treated like that.

Dave and I had spent a lot of time together studying in the dorms. And we'd have devotions together sometimes, and prayed for each other a lot. It felt like I was losing a brother. I didn't see Dave again that day, and knew that for some time, I wouldn't see him again.

That afternoon, I determined that I no longer had a choice. I had to make a change, before all hell broke loose and there was nothing I could do to save myself. I decided I needed to get a part time job, and start saving money. I made an appointment to see Bro Marks about a job the next day.

Chapter Eight:

Finding a Job

Bro Marks was on staff solely to help students find work off campus. I made my way to his office after lunch in order to find a job. Bro Marks was always happy to see a student come down looking for work, and I was quickly welcomed into his office.

"Bro Marks, I was hoping you could help me find a job."

"Certainly Mr Tate, what kind of work do you have experience doing?" he inquired.

"Well, my most recent job I had over the summer was working in a buffet type restaurant, but I've also worked in a butcher shop."

Bro Marks furrowed his eyebrows, and went through a stack of papers on his desk. He finally found what he was looking for, and handed me an application.

"Fill this out, and take it to the New Town Buffet over off of Quince" he said.

"Thank you Bro Marks" I said as I headed for the door.

"It's what I'm here for," he said, "if you have trouble, come back and see me."

I filled out the application in my room, then signed out on my personal sign out sheet in my room and walked out to my car. I drove down to Quince, and asked to see the manager. A few moments later, he came out, and introduced himself as Mike. I handed him the application, and he and I took a seat near the back of the restaurant to talk. He looked over the application as he asked me a few introductory questions.

"So you go to Tennessee Baptist huh?"

"Yes sir I do" I said.

"Well, I won't hold that against you," he said with a grin. I was fairly certain his voice sounded halfway serious the way he made that statement, but I shrugged it off. Pastor Hodge was always talking about how good of a relationship TBBC had with employers in the area, because TBBC students were supposed to be such good workers.

"So you've done this kind of work before?"

"Yes sir, back home."

"What position did you hold there?"

"Well, I started out as hot bar attendant, but within a month I was promoted to head of the hot bar, then I got my certification to be hot cook as well. I also did the salad bar, and was called in to help with prep work and cutting the steaks for steak night."

"Well, it looks like you are definitely qualified for this job. And we can make accommodations around your school schedule, I know TBBC has certain hours you can work and can't work. I'll start you out on the hot bar again, but as fast as you rose at the restaurant back home, you'll likely be promoted soon here as well."

"Thank you sir, I look forward to it."

"Can you start tomorrow?"

65

"Yes sir, I can."

"Okay, I'll put you down to train tomorrow. Let me know when you get here how long you're able to stay."

I went back to the college, relieved I had found work so easily. And I was glad to be able to get to do something I excelled at. Working in the butcher shop had given me a strong work ethic, my boss there had been strict, but fair. He had explained to me the importance of working hard in the real world. My folks had taught me to work, finding me lawns to mow from people in the church. Working at the restaurant, I put all the skills taught me by my parents and my other job to good use, and quickly rose through the ranks. And now, I had the opportunity to do it again at college.

I walked into work the next day, and Mike introduced me to Steve, who was going to train me. Steve and I laughed and joked as we talked about different things throughout the night. As it got closer to closing time, Steve turned to ask me a question.

"So, I hear that you attend TBBC, is that right?"

"Yes, I do" I responded, "you've heard of it?"

He chuckled, "Sure I heard of it, most everybody around here knows the college and church. So do you really like it there?"

I pondered the question for a moment. I had liked it there, before the last couple of weeks. But I wasn't so sure now.

"I'm not sure," I responded, "I did like it there, I'm not so sure now."

Steve just nodded his head, but didn't respond to that. We started cleaning everything up, but a few minutes later, he had another question.

"How long have you been a Christian?"

"You mean how long have I been saved?"

"Yes," he said.

"About a year or so," I responded, "I got saved my freshman year out here. Are you a Christian?"

He chuckled, "Yes, I've been a Christian for a few years. My daddy is a preacher."

"Oh really? My dad is a preacher too."

Steve smiled, "I guess we have more in common than we thought."

When I got back to the dorm that night, I thought long and hard about my conversation with Steve. He didn't look like the kind of Christian I was used to seeing. It occurred to me that I had never asked him what kind of church he attended. I decided to ask him when we worked together next.

Over the next few days, I got to know Steve really well. His dad was a preacher at a Missionary Baptist church. He'd grown up in church his entire life, and got saved when he was a teenager. Steve was working at the restaurant while studying at the local university to become a teacher. I had asked him if his church didn't expect him to be a preacher too. He looked at me rather puzzled at first, and I explained how with many of the churches like the one I grew up in, folks expected you to become a preacher if you were a preacher's kid. He looked at me in amazement, and then responded.

"Brother, there's no reason on earth folks should expect

somebody to become a preacher just because their daddy is a preacher. No, folks don't expect that of me. If God wanted me to become a preacher, then yes, I'd be a preacher. But I feel like God wants me to be a teacher, and teach students here in the city and give them opportunities they need to get ahead in life. And I can be a witness to them by doing that."

I looked at him in surprise. I'd never heard of anything like this before.

"You mean you think God has called you into secular work?"

He looked at the shock on my face and laughed, "Sure, if you wanna call it that. But isn't any work holy if God is putting you there?"

The next day, I thought about Steve's comments during classes. When I thought about it, it made total sense. God doesn't just make people preachers and missionaries, he also makes them teachers and cops and construction workers. As I sat in class that day, I heard Bro Ortiz comment about God calling people to the ministry. I decided to bring up what Steve and I had talked about.

"Bro Ortiz, what about Christians who don't work in the ministry? Doesn't God put them where they are too?"

"Well Jason, that's a good question, but the answer is no. Secular jobs aren't ministry, so God doesn't put people in those jobs. He puts people into the ministry. Now people can be good Christians, and be in a secular job, but God doesn't put them there."

That afternoon, we got notice in our mailboxes that the Soulwinning Conference would be next week. This meant classes would be suspended in place of preaching services, and spending time in the city handing out tracts. I got another letter in my mailbox besides the Conference flier, from Pastor Hodge. Since my dad was one of the speakers at the Conference, I'd been invited to lunch with the conference speakers and their family. I wasn't sure whether to be excited or not.

Chapter Nine:

Dad's Visit

The Soulwinning conference was starting on Monday. Sunday, after the morning service, there was a lunch for the visiting speakers and their families. I was invited, since my father was speaking, so I didn't go back on my bus route. The lunch was held at a local restaurant, where Pastor Hodge would bring visiting pastors.

The lunch went well, the talk was lively as the preachers discussed the upcoming events of the week. The restaurant had set us a room apart from the rest of the establishment. As the afternoon wore on, many of the speakers and their wives left to go back to the hotel and get some rest. Finally, it was down to myself, my dad, and Pastor Hodge.

Dad turned to me, "So, I hear you're working now."

"Yes, I'm working over at a buffet-type restaurant."

Dad nodded his head, "How do you like it?"

"It's good work for right now, plus I get free food on the clock."

Dad and Pastor Hodge broke out laughing. "That's a Baptist for you!" exclaimed PastorHodge.

Then the conversation turned more serious. "So I hear you were dating a girl?"

"Yes" I responded warily. I wondered what was going on now.

"She's a bus kid right?"

"Yes, she is."

"You know son, you've gotta be careful about dating a girl from the bus ministry. I'm not sure that I approve of this. The kids on the bus ministry, thank God they're saved, but they can be a bad influence on kids raised in church."

"I don't understand what her being a bus kid has to do with anything Dad. She loves God, and wants to live her life for him. She acts more like a Christian than some of the guys on my dorm floor."

Dad sighed, "Did you know she's been with other guys before?"

"Yes Dad, I know. She told me already, she thought it was important to tell me."

Pastor Hodge interrupted, "She's already seduced one boy from our church, do you want to be next to fall to her?"

I sat in silence for a few moments. It was bad enough that my dad was on my case about this, but with Pastor Hodge jumping in, it was getting worse.

"Son, as your father, I can tell you that Christina is not God's will for your life."

"All due respect Dad, but you've never met her."

"No, but Pastor Hodge has, and he has told me all about her. She's not the type of girl you should be dating."

"How do you know God's will for my life anyway Dad? Wouldn't God be giving me signs? Wouldn't God speak to me about this?"

Dad's eyes narrowed a bit, and I could see he was becoming angry. But at this point, I didn't care so much. He had attacked Christina, and now I was mad too.

"Son, God is speaking to you. That's why Pastor Hodge and I are telling you about her. She is not the type of girl you need to spend your time with. You will not date her."

"Dad, I don't..."

He cut me off, "That's my final word on the matter son, since you're obviously not listening to what Godly people have told you about this matter, I'm giving the college permission to campus you."

I knew all too well what that meant, I'd not be having any fun for a while. Forget the fact that I was an adult. The colleges in IFB circles don't see their students as adults, but as children who still need parental permission for almost everything. And now my fate was sealed. I was a marked man at the college, and soon every faculty member would know that fact. If I attempted to communicate with Christina, they may very well intercept. I had to move fast.

"When I got back to church that evening, I quickly went to my seat and started writing a note. I knew I had to get it to Christina relatively quickly. I saw Julie come in the back of the auditorium. She and Christina always sat a few rows ahead of me, but Christina's bus came in later, so Julie would be there for a few minutes and I could give her the note.

"Hey Julie, how's it going," I asked.

She glanced around quickly, and I knew she had been told by Christina what was going on. She sat in her pew, and looked up.

"It's going pretty good, how about you?"

I sat my Bible on the pew next to her, with my note slightly sticking out, "I'm doing okay."

She pulled out the note and placed it in her own Bible, "Good, glad to hear it," she said.

With that, I turned and walked back to my pew and sat down. Tony and I talked for a while, mostly about the upcoming conference. I noticed when Christina came in, and saw her sit down up ahead of me. Julie handed her the note, and I saw Christina reading. A few moments later, she turned around and caught my eye. I could see she was troubled by what was now going on, just as I was. The organ and piano began to play, and we knew that was the signal that the service was about to start. I don't remember the sermon that night, but I do remember thinking to myself that something had to be done. I just didn't know what.

The conference began the next day. Pastor Hodge opened up the conference, introducing all the speakers sharing the platform with him. My dad spoke first, and I quickly tuned him out. I'd heard all of his sermons before, and knew it wouldn't be anything different than what I'd heard in the past.

After dad spoke, Dr Wheeler from Texas came up to speak. His sermon was on the spiritual benefits of Soulwinning. Including the notion that a man who is a great soulwinner can get away with sin in his life because of what he is doing for God.

"Young people, you may worry about things you've done in your life that are wrong. But let me tell you, a person who is a soulwinner doesn't have to worry about the sin he committed this morning, because he's a soulwinner. And soulwinners are always blessed by God. Why, just look at King David and King Solomon. Both of those men ran around on their wives, had multiple wives, David committed murder. But they still had God's hand of blessing on their lives. Why? Because they were soulwinners. If you are a soulwinner, you don't have to worry, because you are doing the greatest work there is!"

The "amen corner" was loving this sermon. The howling and amening from that section was loud and almost out of control. I looked up at my dad, and I could see even his face was disturbed by this. But after Dr Wheeler spoke, Pastor Hodge commended him for his sermon. After Dr Wheeler spoke, it was time for lunch, and then off to do some Soulwinning in the city.

Tony and I went and canvassed a street near my own bus route. We led a few people through a tract and a quick prayer, but I felt like we had done them a disservice by not explaining the Gospel fully. I wasn't sure in my own mind that they really understood what we were telling them, but they prayed anyway.

That night at work, I talked to Steve about my being campused. He looked at me in surprise.

"They actually campused you because of who you're dating?"

"Yeah. Well, I guess it's rather who I'm not dating. There is a staff member whose daughter is about my age, and they're wanting to set me up with her, but they can't as long as Christina and I are together. So the easiest way for them to stop us from dating is to forbid us from speaking to each other."

"Man, they have some real control issues there."

"Yeah, I guess they do."

The next day shortly after we got to the church for the conference, Julie came over to where I was sitting. I stiffened for a moment, because talking to her could get me in trouble. But she went to somebody two pews ahead of me to ask them a question. As she did so, I saw her put a note in a hymnal in the pew in front of me. I smiled to myself, she and Christina were being smart about this. After she left, I grabbed the hymnal, and acted as though I were flipping through it until I found the note. I quickly stuffed it into my shirt pocket.

When the service started, I pulled out the note to read.

Dear Jason,

It disturbs me greatly, what is going on around us and what is happening to us. You and I have now both been campused, without doing anything wrong except for not bowing to the will of these men. How can this place call itself a Christian college? I am so ready to leave here now, but I don't want to leave without you. What do we do next?

Love you,

Christina

I sat, pondering the note in my hand. She was scared, and I was worried. I didn't know what to do at this point. The semester had little more than a month left, I needed to figure something out. We did Soulwinning that day in a more upscale part of town. Not many people we ran into were interested or had the time to listen.

When I went to work that night, Mike came out of the office.

"Hey Jason, your college called up here earlier."

I looked at him surprised, "They did?"

"Yes, and they told me if any female students from there come in, you're not allowed to talk to them."

My face flushed with anger, and Mike saw that right off. "Calm down, I'm just messing with you. They didn't call. And if they did, I'd tell them I treat my employees like adults, and not like little children who need hand holding. Are they seriously doing this to you?"

"Yes, they are."

"And it's all because you're dating one person, and they think you should date someone else?"

"Yes."

"Well what gives them the right to make that determination?"

"I'm not sure exactly."

The rest of the night went along smoothly. It was a slow work day, so I didn't have to do much. When my shift ended, I decided to go ask Mike something.

"Hey Mike."

"Yeah, what's up Jason?"

"Do you know of a place where I can get online besides the library? The school has started putting monitors in the library to check up on what we're looking at."

"You're kidding right?"

"No, not at all."

"Come on into the office," he said, "we've got internet access here. What do you need to do?"

"I need to get a couple email addresses and email some people."

I logged on to the BBB, and found the email addresses I needed. I quickly typed out a couple of letters and sent them on their way. One was to Dave, and I hoped he'd check his email soon.

The next day, I didn't work since it was a Wednesday. We had church in the evening, so that afternoon we all stuck around at the school. I had been hanging out in Colonial Court, and decided to head back to my room. As I walked down the hall, I saw Christina emerge from the faculty hallway, with tears in her eyes. Something was wrong, and I was determined to find out what it was.

Chapter Ten:

The Deadly Sin of Gossip

That Saturday, I was sick and unable to go out on my bus route. So I sat in the dorm, and read and studied while I lay there doing nothing. After a few hours, my cell phone rang. Only a few people had my number, so I checked the caller ID first to see who it was. It wasn't a number I knew, but I answered it anyway.

"Hello?"

"Hey Jason, it's me, Christina."

"Christina?!"

"Try not to sound so shocked," she giggled.

"Where are you calling from?"

"I stopped by mom's house. I thought I'd call you direct, rather than go through the switchboard. I heard you were sick today?"

"Yeah, I'm not feeling too well, but I am better than I was this morning."

"That's good, I'm glad you're feeling a little better. I hope you feel better soon."

"Me too. So how have you been?"

"I'm doing good. Except, I've been taken off work scholarship."

"They took you off work scholarship?! Why?"

"They said that they have too many people in the program right now, and they needed to cut a few out."

"Is that why you were crying the other day?"

"Yes, but it's not so much that I'm crying over losing the work scholarship, as it is that I'm afraid that I'll have to leave and lose you."

"You're not going to lose me Christina. I promise." I said. And I meant it, there was no way Christina and I were going to be split up by the college. I was determined not to let this happen.

"Thanks Jason, it makes me feel better to hear it from your voice. I just wish I could hear your voice more often."

"And I wish I could hear yours."

We talked for a few minutes longer. When we hung up the phone, even though I was sick, I still felt immensely better than I had before. I walked down to the laundry room, and started washing some laundry. While I was there, I saw security come down the stairs and walk toward Jake's room. They left with several papers in their hands, and walked back up the stairs and out of the dorm.

When Jake got in that night, later than everybody else, I pulled him aside to talk to him.

"Dude, what's going on? Security was in your room today."

He looked around, "Amy's being expelled."

"Why?"

He sighed and looked down, "She's been messing around with drugs."

"How long have you known?"

His face turned red, "I've known for a while. I even tried some when she offered me."

"Why is only she getting in trouble?"

"C'mon, you know why," he responded.

I nodded my head, he was right, I did know. As would anybody else. His dad was on staff, Jake wasn't about to get in any serious trouble.

The next day I was able to go to church since I was feeling better. All the college students were buzzing about Amy's sudden expulsion. It seemed like everybody knew the story, it had spread more quickly than I had imagined. And most students knew about Jake's involvement.

Monday in chapel, Dr Towler stood up to give the sermon. He started off talking in very broad terms about a rumor that had been going around campus the past few days.

"Students, I realize that speculation is a part of human nature. And you're looking at this situation, and wondering what exactly is going on. I understand that some of you have been told certain things. But let me warn you, if you continue repeating these things, you will be expelled for being a gossip. You're not just playing at telling stories here, you're messing with a man's ministry. Gossip will not be tolerated in this school."

I can't say that this sermon was entirely unexpected by the majority of the student body. Naturally, the administration would want to squelch any rumors floating around, whether true or untrue. It reminded me of the Wizard of Oz, the part where the great Oz shouts "Pay no attention to the man behind the curtain."

"Gossip is a deadly sin, which will ruin the lives and souls of many! Suppose that you ruin the ministry of some great man of God because you believed the word of a harlot over the word of a preacher! Be not deceived young people! If you continue to gossip, slander, or mock the man of God, God Himself will judge you! 2Ki 2:23-24 And he went up from thence unto Bethel: and as he was going up by the way, there came forth little children out of the city, and mocked him, and said unto him, Go up, thou bald head; go up, thou bald head. And he turned back, and looked on them, and cursed them in the name of the LORD. And there came forth two she bears out of the wood, and tore forty and two children of them. Beware of the she bears students!

I knew the term she bears was a warning that God would punish those who said anything negative about the man of God. I'd heard the warning before in sermons, but never had it sounded so silly. The whole place reeked of hypocrisy, and I knew that there wasn't much more I could have to do with this college.

Chapter Eleven

Thanksgiving Break

Thanksgiving break was finally almost here. Like most students, I was heading home for a couple days of relaxation. It was two days before break, and the air was filled with expectancy for what was ahead. I walked to my mailbox and opened it up. Much to my surprise, it contained a letter from my sister.

My sister was the black sheep of the family. She was about two years younger than me, and had just turned eighteen. She had not been home in a few years, and hardly ever wrote me. Dad and mom had sent her to the "Miklat Home for Girls" a few hundred miles away from home. Sarah had been romantically involved with our choir director when she was thirteen. When she got pregnant, dad shipped her off to the home for girls so nobody would know what had happened. Our choir director conveniently moved out of state and nary a word was said to the church he was now working for. Sarah's baby was put up for adoption, although she had wanted desperately to keep him.

Sarah hadn't written me at all ever since I had started going to TBBC, and mom and dad never spoke of her. So naturally, I was curious as to why she would write me after all this. I took the letter down to my room.

Dear Jason,

I know it's been a long time since I've written, and I'm sorry. I guess I've been resentful toward you because you've gotten to stay home while I've had to come here to Miklat. I'm writing you this letter, and sending it from some people in town who I know and trust. Mom and dad won't come to get me from Miklat, and I'm having to stay. I'm eighteen now, I should be gone. I've seen other girls turn eighteen and their parents come to get them, but not me. Mom and dad say they're not going to get me if I don't change my attitude. But Jason, they don't

84

understand. It's hell here. And I don't mean that in a cursing kind of way, but it is as close to hell as anything I've ever seen. If we don't do what we're told, we got locked in a room and are forced to listen to sermons for days at a time. I've been praying for so long that God would get me out of here, but He hasn't heard me yet. Sometimes I wonder if he's even there. The food here is horrible. I know that you probably wouldn't understand Jason, but I desperately need to get out of here. And you're the only one I can turn to right now. I don't even know why I'm writing to you, except for some reason I thought maybe you'd understand and would help me. And even if you don't think you can help me, please don't show this letter to mom and dad. I'm terrified of what would happen if they discovered I'm writing you. They promised to come visit for Thanksgiving. I hope you'll be there.

     Your sister,

     Sarah

     I could feel my heart grow heavy with sorrow. I had never realized that my sister had been in that much agony there. I used to think she had brought all this on herself. Now, I wasn't as sure as I had been. I determined to talk to her over Thanksgiving break and see what I could do for her.

     The next day, everybody was chattering in the cafeteria. Everybody was eager and ready to leave for an extended weekend. I was sitting around with the guys, telling tall tales of hunting trips we'd taken on Thanksgivings past. We were all talking excitedly, and then Tony looked over at my plate with a grin.

     "Hey Jason, you gonna eat that pie or what?"

"Nah, you can have it, come around and get it."

Tony came around the table and reached for my pie. I grabbed the back of his head as he bent over and pushed his face right into the pie. All the guys started whooping and laughing. Tony grabbed a napkin and started wiping off his face and walking away. Then he noticed a pie on the table behind me and grabbed it while my back was turned.

"Hey Jason," he said.

I turned to look and promptly got a face full of pumpkin pie. By now the dining hall was filled with laughter from even staff as Tony and I wiped pie from our faces. Tony and I laughed together as we looked at each other's pie smeared faces. That night, we all stayed up late talking about our upcoming break. We went to bed in the early morning hours, exhausted, but glad to be out for a few days.

I loaded my car in the morning, and drove off of campus. Finally, I had a couple of days away from school to try and think things through clearly. After I got a couple hours away from school, Christina called.

"Hey Jason, you on your way home?"

"Yes, I should be there in another couple hours."

"What are your plans?"

"Well, tomorrow we're going to see my sister over in Ohio."

I proceeded to tell Christina about Sarah and her problems. Christina listened as I told her all about the letter and my sister's plea for help.

"Oh Jason, that sounds awful. I feel so bad for her. Why didn't your dad go to the police?"

"I don't know. I don't know why he does anything he does."

"Well, I hope you can help her Jason."

"Me too."

"Well, I guess I better let you go so you can drive safely."

"Hey, Christina, what are you doing Monday morning?"

"Nothing, why?"

"I might come back a few hours early, and I thought we could meet someplace and talk."

"Okay, um, I guess we can talk later? You can call me when you're on your way back."

"Okay, I'll talk to ya then."

"Alright, bye."

"Bye Chrissy, love ya."

"Love you too."

We hung up and I drove on for a while in silence. I didn't know what to do about Sarah. I had an idea about me and Christina, but I knew I had to take care of Sarah too. Mom and dad weren't going to help her, of that I was sure.

Mom and dad were glad to see me when I finally pulled into the driveway. We sat and talked for a while, until I finally got too tired to keep talking.

"I'm gonna turn in folks, I'm tired, it's been a long day."

"Alright son," said Dad, "sleep well, see you in the morning."

Mom took a glass of water into my room and sat it on my night stand. "Night son."

"Night mom, see you on the flip side."

The next day we got into Dad's car, and drove across the state to a small border town where the Miklat Home was located. Thanksgiving dinner there was small, and most of the girls were pretty quiet and didn't talk much. Sarah caught my eye a couple times during the dinner, and I could see she was anxious to talk to me. Most of the other girls parents' hadn't come for dinner, and it was easy to see they were upset about the fact. After dinner, Mom and Dad got to talking with the other parents and the leadership there at the girls home. Sarah and I went outside to talk.

"Jason, you've gotta help me get out of here," she said, her eyes pleading with me.

"Sarah, there's only so much I can do right now. I haven't got much money, and I want to get married soon, but I promise you, I'll help you get out of here."

"You're getting married? Mom and Dad didn't say anything about that!"

"Well, they don't know."

I hesitated, then began telling Sarah all about Christina and I. I told her everything, from our talks with the school leadership, to what Dad had said at the dinner that day. I could see Sarah was upset about what was happening to us.

"Why would they do that to you?"

"I don't know Sarah. How much longer do you think you can last here? Until the end of the semester?"

"Yes, I can wait it out that long here."

"Okay, when this semester is over, I'm gonna get you out of here. You need to be ready to leave at a minute's notice. The semester is over in just a couple weeks."

She looked at me eagerly, "Okay, I'll be ready. I promise."

"Is there a way I can get ahold of you?"

Sarah wrote down a phone number, "I bought a disposable phone that I keep hidden and on silent. Call the number and leave a voice mail."

"Okay, I will definitely do that sis."

Just then another girl came out of the main building. She was young looking, with brown hair done up into braids. She reminded me of a girl from the nineteenth century with her plain cotton dress and plain features.

"Sarah, Jason, you're parents want you inside."

"Alright Gabe, we're coming."

Sarah looked up at me and said quietly, "Be careful around Gabe, she's not good at keeping secrets, and might rat me out in order to get extra privileges."

I smiled, "Don't worry sis, I know how to watch my back."

We walked back inside together, and mingled for a while longer with everybody else. At the end of the day, I gave her a hug and told her goodbye. Mom and Dad gave her a hug too, but it seemed more out of obligation than anything else. From what I had seen that day, I knew I needed to get Sarah out of there and soon.

Chapter Twelve:

Secrets

When I got back to Memphis, I gave Christina a call. We decided to meet over at my job. We could grab something to eat back in the employee training section and not have to worry about being spotted. Mike welcomed the two of us, and gave me an approving nod after looking at Christina.

Christina and I got some food, then went into the party room which was normally set aside for employee training. We sat down, and started discussing what had happened over Thanksgiving break. Christina's mom had disappeared again, which meant that she had probably gone on a drug binge and wouldn't be around for a few weeks. I told her about Sarah, and what was going on with her. Christina was shocked that somebody could be treated in that manner.

"How could they do that to her? Don't your parents love her?"

"Yes, but they think this is what's best for her."

"Wow Jason, just wow. I've never heard of people doing that to their children. They aren't able to discipline their children themselves and so they ship them off to have somebody else do the dirty work?"

"Something like that I guess. Although with some, it's to try to keep them away from the wrong kind of friends. Mostly kids who do drugs."

"So what are you going to do about her?"

"Well, hopefully at the end of the semester I'll get her out of there."

"How are you going to do that?"

"Well...Christina, I was thinking..." my voice trailed off for a moment as I struggled to find the right words to say to her.

"Yes?" she said, "What were you thinking?"

Her brown eyes looked into mine, and I looked away for a moment.

"Well, what if...what if we got married at the end of the semester, and picked up Sarah and took her to live with us for a while?"

I saw the surprise register in her eyes. "What did you just say Jason?"

I dropped down to one knee and pulled out my high school class ring. "Will you marry me Christina?"

I saw her eyes fill with tears. I knew my whole world depended on her next words. I could feel the knots in my stomach tightening.

"Yes, OH YES!" She almost shouted, "Oh Jason! Yes!"

She started laughing as she took my class ring. She took off her necklace, and put my ring on the chain.

"I'll wear this next to my heart until we're free." she said.

We sat and talked for a while longer, as I shared some ideas with her. But both of us were focused on what I had just happened. We were going to get married, forget what the college said. I knew this was the right thing for the two of us. Just a few more weeks, and it would all be over for us.

The next day at college started out well. Although we still weren't able to talk to each other, I had a good day talking to the guys I knew about what we had done over our short vacation. I decided against mentioning my engagement to Christina to anybody.

Work that night went well. I told Mike and Steve about my engagement. They both congratulated me.

"So when are you getting married" asked Steve.

"As soon as the semester ends. It's just a matter of finding a place to get married....a quick wedding you know. There's nobody we really want to invite, considering our situations."

"Well I understand that," said Mike, "but you do need

witnesses buddy. Hey, how about Steve and I tag along?"

"Well, yeah, that sounds like a good idea."

We talked some more for a while, and I sent some emails out to my friends from the BBB and Dave in particular. I got back home at the end of the night, and drifted off to sleep while trying to decide exactly what our plan was. I had a pretty good idea of what I was doing, it was just a matter of the details.

That weekend, I headed out for bus calling. While my bus worker and I were knocking on doors inviting the kids to church, Christina called me up. I hung up the phone and told my bus worker I had to run back to work and drop off some keys I had forgotten to leave the night before. He gave me a strange look as I left, but I shrugged it off, figuring he was just wondering why I would run back just for that. I didn't get back to my bus route for two hours, but my bus worker still said nothing. The next Monday, I got a call to Pastor Hodge's office.

"Jason, where did you go Saturday?"

"What's that?"

"When you left your bus route in the middle of bus calling, where did you go?"

"I left to drop off some keys for my manager."

"I was at the restaurant Saturday, I never saw you."

I felt my heart drop for a moment. Did he know what was going on somehow?

"I went in the back way sir."

"Will your manager confirm that for me?"

"Yes sir, he will."

"What's your manager's name?"

"Mike." I responded, getting uncomfortable with all the questions.

Pastor Hodge picked up the phone, and called up the restaurant. He asked for Mike, and when Mike got on, he asked him whether or not I had come back to drop off keys at the restaurant, and if I had come in the back. When Mike answered affirmatively, I saw Pastor Hodge's face turn red.

"If I find out you're lying, none of our students will ever work for you again!" He slammed down the receiver. Pastor Hodge looked at me, his face red. He was angry, and I could tell.

"Have you and Christina been communicating in some form since I've told you not to talk with her?"

My mind raced with all the possibilities that existed. Perhaps the notes had been found, or maybe Tony mentioned that I was upset about not being able to talk with her. I decided to go with the truth.

"Yes sir, we have."

The surprise on his face told me that he wasn't expecting me to answer this way, but he looked at me and smirked.

"Yes, I know," he said, "Julie has been good enough to come forward and tell us what has been going on."

"Julie?" I couldn't wrap my mind around this. Why would Julie say anything about this mess?

"Yes, Julie. She's told us that both of you have been passing notes through her for some time now. We found a couple of those notes too. I must tell you Jason, I'm very disappointed in you. But I promise

94

you this, you'll not be doing this again."

My puzzled look on my face caused him to smirk yet again. "Christina no longer attends here. As of today, she is no longer a student of TBBC."

I felt my blood run cold. Christina was no longer a student there? This meant I'd not get to see her as often over the next couple of weeks until we got married. But we would certainly be able to keep in touch I reasoned.

"Jason, you're no longer allowed to have a cell phone on campus. And your driving privileges are now restricted. You may go to work directly, and back. You may not drive into Memphis on the weekends for any reason. You will drive with someone else, and go on your bus route. You're not going to have the same freedom you had before Jason."

"Yes sir," I responded. I didn't really know what else to say. I handed over my cell phone after locking the keypad and turning it off. Then I headed back to my class. I walked by security helping Christina remove her things from the campus. I could see she was upset, but she looked at me for a moment as if to tell me she'd be waiting to talk to me when I could get a hold of her. I smiled to myself, they only thought they were splitting us up.

Chapter Thirteen:

Tragedy Strikes

The guys at work were shocked when I told them what had happened at college that day. None of them could believe what I had told them. The idea that such a thing could happen was completely shocking to them.

"Can they do that to you?" asked Mike.

"Yeah, I guess. I mean, we did sign a statement that we would obey all the rules of the college when we signed on."

"But is that legal though? I mean, they can take your cell phone away? I can understand them taking away your privileges, or kicking you out, but taking your stuff away from you?"

"I dunno. I guess it is."

"Man, that's rather harsh. I mean, doing something like this just because they don't like the girl you're dating. It's just not right."

"Yeah, I know."

I spent most of the night wondering about Christina. I tried to call her up a couple of times, but got no answer from her home phone. After we closed down that night, I walked outside toward my car, wishing I had parked closer as it was starting to rain.

"Jason!"

I turned and looked, Christina was standing over at the corner of the building.

"Nobody's here, I checked" she said.

I ran over to her. "What are you doing out here? You're going to catch a cold out in the rain like this" I scolded.

She looked up at me "Mama lost the house, I don't really have anywhere to go right now."

I paused for a moment, "Hold on, I'll be right back."

I ran back inside the restaurant and found Steve. "Hey Steve, do you think you and your folks could do me a favor?"

"Sure bro, what's up?"

I quickly related to him about Christina, and told him about how she had nowhere to go right now.

"You got it bro," he said, "I'm getting off right now, I'll be right out."

I walked back outside and grabbed Christina's hand. "Hey, I found someplace for you to go. My friend Steve who works here, his dad is a preacher, they can let you stay at their place until we get all this worked out."

"I don't want to put anyone out" she said.

I looked down at her, smiled and kissed her lips. "Don't worry hon, everything will be alright, you're not putting anybody out. I promise you, everything's going to be better soon"

She smiled and drew closer to me and we hugged. "Everything's going to be alright," I said, "I promise."

"How?" she asked, "How do you know everything is going to be okay? Jason, I have no money, I have nowhere to live, I have nowhere to work. I just have what I left college with..." Her voice trailed off, and I could see tears welling up in her eyes again. "I'm scared Jason, I'm scared nothing is ever going to be okay again. Mom's not been perfect, but she needs help, and I don't know what to do to help her. We have to get her help Jason."

"Christina, I promise you, everything is going to be okay. If I have to take the college apart brick by brick, I will make everything okay for you again. God isn't going to leave us out here by ourselves. Just a couple more weeks, and we'll be far away from here. I'll talk to some people I know, see if we can get your mom in a drug rehab clinic. We're all family, we'll take care of her, just like we'll take care of my sister. Don't forget that babe. "

Steve came out, "Hey."

"Hey Steve," I said, "I want you to meet Christina. Christina, this is Steve."

"Hi," said Christina shyly.

"Hello," said Steve, flashing a smile. "It's great to finally meet you, Jason talks about you all the time."

Christina blushed and giggled nervously. "Only good things I hope."

"Only good things," said Steve grinning, "And all the time, over and over and over and over."

"Hey," I said, "She's not all I talk about."

"True," said Steve, "You also talk about things pertaining to Christina."

I jokingly punched his shoulder. Steve ran out to his car, and drove it up by the building so Christina didn't have to walk all the way out in the rain.

"I'll talk to you later Christina, Steve will take care of you, he's a good guy."

"Bye Jason, be careful."

"I will be."

Steve and Christina drove off down the road, leaving me in the rain. I walked back to my car, pondering the evenings events. I had to do something about this, I just wasn't sure what to do or how to go about taking care of the matter. I hopped in my car, and headed back toward the college. The roads were slick as the unusually cold weather was causing them to ice a little. I wasn't unaccustomed to driving on snow and ice, so it wasn't bothering me much, but I did take it slow. As

I drove down the highway, I noticed a couple of accidents on the other side of the road. I saw the brake lights farther ahead of me turning red, so I started putting on my brakes as well. All of the sudden, I heard a horn honking loudly, followed by a brilliant flash of light and everything going black.

Chapter Fourteen:

Tragedy Strikes

Mike called up Steve the next morning to tell him Jason was in the hospital after having an accident. Steve was hesitant to tell me outright at first. Then he told me that Jason had been in an accident with a tractor trailer. The car was totaled, and Jason was completely unconscious. The news crushed me, and I didn't know what to do. I begged Steve to drive me to the hospital, and we finally got there at noon. I ran into the hospital, up to the nurse's station.

"What room is Jason Tate in?" I asked breathlessly.

The nurse looked up at me, then to her computer. "He's in room 309, go down the hall, and take a right to get to the elevator."

"Thank you," I said as I rushed down the hall. I got to the elevator, and pushed the button for the third floor repeatedly until the doors closed. Steve was downstairs parking the car, but I couldn't wait for him. When the elevator got to the third floor, I almost knocked several people over trying to get out of the door. I saw a couple of people from TBBC down the hall by Jason's room, and Jason's dad talking to Pastor Hodge and the doctor, but this time I didn't care. I walked down the hall to his room.

"Christina, you can't come in," said Pastor Hodge.

"You can't tell me what to do Pastor Hodge," I said sarcastically, "I don't go to your school any more remember?"

Mr. Tate stepped forward, "I'm sorry, but I can't allow you into my son's room. Family only is allowed in here."

He turned to the doctor and told the doctor to go ahead with the surgery they were planning. My face flushed with anger, and I decided to go ahead and lay it all out.

"I'm sorry Mr Tate, but I'm not leaving. And doctor, I don't believe you can perform any surgery without notifying the immediate next of kin."

Everybody paused for a moment and looked at me. "I'm sorry, what was that?" said Mr Tate, his face turning red with anger.

I looked at the doctor, "Doctor, can you and I talk in private?"

The doctor hesitated, and looked at the men first, then back at me. "Sure, let's step down the hallway here."

He and I stepped back near the third floor nurse's station. "Doctor, my name is Christina Tate, I'm Jason's wife. We've just been married." I reached into my purse to pull out the certificate and showed it to him. "I'd like to know what is going on with him right now."

My mind flashed back to the week before. I called up Jason while he was on his bus route, and we were going over to Arkansas to get a marriage license to fill out. He picked me up, and we found a cute

102

little courthouse in a small town across the border. The court clerk asked us if we wanted to get married right then. We looked at each other for a moment, and Jason looked at her and said yes. The judge was a sweet, older man; and the court clerk acted as our witness. We decided not to leave the college right away, so we'd have enough money to run up and get Jason's sister when we left. Jason said he had already found a place for us to move to when we got out. And now he was laying in a hospital bed, possibly dying.

The doctor looked at the certificate for a moment, then back to me. "Yes ma'am. Jason has been pretty seriously injured by the accident he was in. We've got him stable, and I think he may make it, but he's got a few cracked ribs, and seems to have some minor bleeding in his skull. We've already taken care of the ribs, but we need to cut into his skull in order to relieve the pressure on his skull. He should be fine after doing so but there's no guarantee. If we don't do this, he won't pull out of this state he's in and will die soon. I also want to cut open his abdomen in order to get a closer look at something." The doctor showed me the scans they had taken, "This dark spot here by the liver may indicate some bleeding, or it could be just a shadow. But I do want to check it out and make sure his liver isn't in any danger. I'm going to need you to sign some forms."

I nodded my head, a little numb at everything that was going on. "Okay," I said, "Can I see him before you go into surgery?"

"Yes," said the doctor, "Do you know if Jason has any medical insurance?"

"Yes, he just got some through his job, covering both of us. I have the card." I reached into my purse and pulled out my wallet, "Here you go."

The doctor gave the card to the nurse outside the door. "I know this is hard for you, but I think he's going to be fine once we get this taken care of. He's a strong young man."

The doctor and I walked back to Jason's room, where Jason's dad again tried to block the door. I had explained to the doctor about our situation, and asked him for his help. The doctor looked at Mr Tate for a moment, and then spoke.

"Mr Tate, I'm going to have to ask you to move."

"She's not getting in to see my son!"

"I'm sorry sir, you don't have any say over that, she is married to your son and that makes her the next of kin."

"What!?" roared Jason's dad, "She is not married to my son!"

"Sir, I've seen the marriage certificate, they are married."

I could see the anger and disapproval on the face of Jason's father, and on Pastor Hodge. "Sir, if you don't get out of the way, I'm going to call for security" said the doctor.

He stepped out of the way, and the doctor and I walked through the door. Jason's dad grabbed my wrist, and turned me around.

"You are not a member of this family!" he growled. "I warned you to stay away from my son."

I pulled my wrist away and walked over by Jason's bed where his mother was. She looked up at me, and I saw the surprise on her face, and she looked at her husband.

"She says she's married to Jason" said Mr Tate.

She looked at me in shock, then down at Jason, and back at me. The look on her face was the same as her husband's. It terrified me, I had no idea what these people would do. I had offended them first by dating their son, then marrying him behind their back. I was relieved to see Steve walk in the room. The doctor was making a call for surgery prep to be done. He turned around and looked at everybody in the room.

"I'm going to have to ask everybody except for Christina to leave right now, they're getting ready to take him down to surgery."

I was only slightly aware of everyone leaving the room. I took Jason's hand in my own, and caught a sob in my throat as I looked at his banged-up face. I felt a tear run down my cheek as I began speaking to him.

"Hey baby, I know you can't hear me. Or maybe you can, I don't know. But I'm here. And it's my turn to be the strong one, okay? I know you're in there. Somewhere. You just can't talk to me right now. But that's okay. The doctor says everything is going to be fine. They're just going to do a little surgery to make you better. And then we can be together okay?"

The orderlies came in and prepared to push him out. I stroked Jason's hand for a moment.

"Okay baby, they're taking you now. You're going into surgery. Remember that I love you okay?" I leaned over and kissed him. "I love you baby, I wish you could talk to me right now, but that's okay."

As I prepared to let go of his hand, I felt a little squeeze. And then the tears began to fall like rain as the orderlies wheeled him down to surgery. Steve came in and gave me a hug. Then we walked down to surgery together. Jason's parents sat on the other side of the waiting room and glared at me. Pastor Hodge had gone back to the college. The doctor had told me the surgery would take a couple of hours, so I grabbed Steve, and took him into the hallway.

"Can you do me a favor?"

"Sure, what do you need?"

"Jason's stuff. I think we need to get it out of the college before it gets thrown out."

"How can I get it out? Won't they stop me?"

"They'll try, but I'm going to write up a note for you so they have to let you in to get his stuff. All of his books have his name in them on the 33rd page."

"Why the 33rd?"

"Jason says it's to remind him of the Trinity. That and most people look for names on the inside cover. This way, it's harder to steal his books. Also, ask Pastor Hodge for his cell phone, they took Jason's cell phone away. Here, I'll write a list."

I hurriedly wrote down a list of things I knew belonged to Jason, and gave it to Steve. "This is his stuff. His roommates may tell you which stuff is his, they may not. But all of Jason's stuff should have his name on it."

Steve got ready to walk off just as a police officer came walking up to us. "I was told you're the wife of Jason Tate?"

"Yes sir," I said, "what can I do for you?"

106

"I realize this may be a bad time for you ma'am, but I need to talk to you about the accident."

Steve looked at me, and I just nodded to him and he took off.

"Yes sir, that's okay."

"Well, from what we've been able to gather from witness statements and everything, it seems your husband was traveling safely. He was hit from behind by trucker who wasn't paying enough attention to the road. Your husband is lucky to be alive, I've seen people killed in accidents like this before."

"So what happens now?"

"Well, the driver who hit him is currently in jail. I've got his insurance information here for you, and they will be reimbursing you and your husband for all your medical expenses. You can sue if you want to, but that advice didn't come from me."

"Yes sir."

"A piece of advice ma'am, the insurance company will be coming to you trying to settle everything with you as quickly as possible. My advice is to consult a lawyer before taking any settlement. Your husbands auto insurance company will probably provide you with a lawyer."

"Yes sir, thank you."

"I hope his surgery goes well ma'am."

The officer walked off after handing me copies of all the paperwork. I walked back into the waiting room and sat down to read through everything. I felt so exhausted, even though I'd only been there for a short time. This was all too much to deal with. I wanted Jason to come and make it all better. The thought made the tears fall again.

I decided to walk down to the hospital chapel. I walked in and there was no one around. I found a pew down front, and began to cry as I talked to God.

Dear God, it's me, Christina. I need your help right now in a big way. Jason's hurt, and I don't want to lose him. I love him so much God, just please, don't take him away from me. I know whatever your will is will happen. But I can't help being selfish about this God. Jason is all I've got in this world right now. I know that you can take and give, but God, let him live.

I rose up from the pew, and walked back out of the chapel. I felt better, having talked to God about what was going on right then. I always had felt better when I talked to God about something, and this was no different. I knew that God had heard me, and deep down I just knew everything was going to be okay.

After waiting for what seemed like an eternity, the doctor came into the waiting room. He motioned for me to follow him, and we stepped out into the hallway.

"Well, the surgery was a success. We've caused the swelling in the brain to lessen and stop, and there was no bleeding from the liver. He should be waking up from surgery soon, you can go in and see him."

I was almost ecstatic, Jason was going to be okay, and he would be awake soon. The doctor motioned for a moment.

"Do you want me to tell his parents?"

"Yes, if you would, please."

With that, the doctor walked into the waiting room, and I took off down the hallway to see Jason. I pulled a chair next to his bed, and grabbed his hand while I looked at him. His color was better, but still, his face was bruised from the impact of the night before. He started stirring a little, and I began talking to him again.

"Hey baby, it's Chrissy, how are you feeling? You just got out of surgery you know. You look a little rough, but you know I love you anyway. Are you ready to wake up yet? Hmm? Well, you need to. I need to talk to you, we have things to talk about okay? So anytime you're ready, go ahead and wake up for me."

I sat there for a few more minutes, and I could see Mr and Mrs Tate standing in the doorway looking on at us. Jason stirred again, and I heard him moan softly. Then I saw his eyes flicker, and then open. His glance first went over to the door where his parents were, then over to me. He smiled wryly, then spoke.

"I guess they know now huh?"

"Yeah baby, they know."

"What'd they say?"

"Don't ask," I responded.

He smiled a bit. Then he looked back over at the doorway. His parents were gone. Steve came walking in the room.

"Hey, Jason! You're okay!"

"Yeah, if you call getting run over by a truck and laying in a hospital bed 'okay'" he responded.

"I saw your parent's go walking down the hall, did they talk to you?"

"No, I guess they're kind of upset." he said

"Well, I got all your stuff out of that college. I think. I'm not totally sure about it all."

"How did you get on campus?" asked Jason

"Christina wrote me a note."

Jason looked back up at me and smiled. "You think of everything don't you Chrissy?"

"I try baby, but I was so scared."

His face got serious, and he gripped my hand. "There's no way I was going to leave you alone, you know that right?"

"I know baby, but I was still scared," I said. I leaned over and gave him a kiss. "I love you."

"I love you too." he said.

The doctor came walking in, and started looking at Jason's vitals.

"Okay folks," he said, "I'm going to have to ask everybody to leave right now so he can get his rest." he looked at me, "You can come back anytime you want, I just want him to go ahead and get some sleep, and likely that won't happen if you're in here with him."

"Okay," I said. "I need to do some stuff anyway. I'll see you later baby."

"See you later," said Jason.

I walked back out to the car with Steve. We drove back to his parents place, and unloaded Jason's stuff into the basement where we could store it for a while. I took Jason's phone and turned it on so I could use it if I needed. I realized that I needed to get a job, so we could have some money when Jason got back out of the hospital.

"Steve, do you think I could get a job over there at the restaurant?"

"Sure, we can go over to the restaurant right now and talk to Mike if you want."

"I'd like that. Then I need to get back to the hospital and sit with Jason."

"Alright, let's go."

Mike and I talked for a little bit, and he was more than willing to give me a job so we could have some money coming in while Jason was out. Mike told me some of the girls at the restaurant had been wanting to give me a wedding shower so Jason and I would have some basic things to start out with. So we talked about a date for that to happen. After we got done talking, Steve drove me back to the hospital. I got back to Jason's room, and sat there beside him and held his hand. He looked so frail there in the hospital bed, lines going from his body to different machines. He just didn't look as big and strong as I knew him to be. The nurse had brought me an extra pillow and blanket so I could sleep in there. I lay my head on the pillow and cried myself to sleep. I needed him so much.

Chapter Fifteen:

Jason Awakes

I woke up later that night, feeling a little bit of pain in my side, but nothing major. I instinctively pressed the little button that would give me some more pain medicine. I opened my eyes, and could see Christina laying in a chair beside me, sleeping peacefully. Even in the glow of hospital light, she was beautiful, and I knew I was lucky to have her by my side.

When Christina woke in the morning, I was already awake and

watching her sleeping. She looked over at me, and smiled.

"Hey, good morning, how are you feeling today?" she asked.

I smiled back at her, "A little better. Still hurting, but I'm feeling a little stronger."

She brushed my hair back and kissed my forehead "They shaved part of your head here you know."

"I know," I said, feeling the spot where I bandage now was noting the absence of hair.

"I got a job at the restaurant, at least until you're strong enough to go back to work."

"Mike's putting you to work huh?"

"Yes, I start tomorrow."

I looked up at her, "I'm sorry things turned out this way Chrissy."

"It's not your fault baby, and things will be better this way. You'll see. Oh, Steve's parents are going to let you stay there too when you get stronger and are able to get out of the hospital."

"Have you seen my parents since yesterday?" I asked.

She hesitated, "No baby, I'm sorry."

We talked for a while longer. Christina had so many ideas of what we could do after I got out of the hospital. We laughed and talked about different things for a little while, and then my parents suddenly came in the door. I could see Christina was slightly flustered at their appearance.

"Hello Mom, Dad."

"Hello son," said Dad. I could see he was upset that Christina was there.

Mom came over and grabbed my hand, "How are you feeling today?"

"Still a little tired, but I'm feeling better."

"So son, when did you get married without telling us?"

"Just a week and a half ago dad."

"And what makes you think this was the right thing for you to do." said Dad.

"Not here dad, this isn't the place for this."

"No, it's exactly the place for this. She has no business being here."

"She has every right to be here dad, she's my wife."

"She'll not be in here for much longer."

"What did you do dad?"

"You'll find out soon enough."

"What do you think you're doing dad?"

"What needs to be done son. If you can't do it yourself, we're going to do it for you."

"You can't do this!" I protested "This isn't right dad."

"Until we get this marriage annulled, this is what has to be done."

"You're doing no such thing dad!" I said angrily.

"Son, you're not thinking clearly right now," Mom said "don't worry, let us take care of everything."

"No! You guys can't do this!" I started yelling at them angrily.

Nurses and doctors came rushing down the hall as I got into a shouting match with my parents. Christina was standing back in the corner crying. I could hear one of the doctors calling for security. Security got into the room and started clearing everyone out.

"Come on everybody, you need to leave. Nobody in here right now. Everybody out, let's go!" barked one of the guards. "Come on, everybody out!"

I lay there in my bed and prayed for a while.

God, it's me. Christina and I need some help right now. I don't know how we're going to get out of this mess God. This is a big deal. Christina's upset, and I don't want her to be upset. I'm not able to do anything, because I'm in the hospital. I need Your help to get through this. Please, give Christina some peace in this, so she isn't more upset than she already is. Help my parents to understand God. Help us all to move past this. Amen.

Later in the afternoon, I heard a knock at my door, and saw Julie peeking around the corner. I could see she was a little nervous and hesitant about being there.

"Come in," I said.

"Hi," she said, trying to work up the courage to look at me, "I wanted to tell you why I did what I did."

"You don't have to do that Julie," I said.

"But I want to," she said, "I need to tell you what happened."

She sat down beside me, and told me about how the college had threatened her with expulsion if she didn't tell them what was going on between Christina and me. She was on one of the tour groups, and her fiancé was there at college too. She didn't have any choice in what

115

she did.

"I'm so sorry Jason, I didn't mean to hurt you guys, I just . . . I couldn't let myself be thrown out."

"It's okay Julie, Christina and I understand. We don't hate you for what happened. It's not your fault."

"Anyway," she said, "I'm leaving the college, I can't stay there anymore. Not after today."

"What happened?" I asked.

She hesitated for a moment, "You were the sermon in chapel today. Pastor Hodge talked about how you are 'being judged by God' for not obeying the administration. Christina was the main subject of the sermon, but you were in it too."

I laughed, "I don't suppose they taped it did they?"

"No, Pastor Hodge ordered them not to tape the sermon."

We talked for a few moments more, and then she left. I called Christina up after, and told her what had happened. Christina told me about her day at work, and told me that Mike had an idea of getting around the restraining order. After talking for a while, we both hung up the phone. I lay back in my bed, exhausted by the events of the day. I drifted off to sleep, hoping the next day would be better.

I was feeling better after a few days, and the doctor said I was well enough to go home. I'd be staying in the apartment above the garage of Steve's parents, but I didn't mind. I did feel like I was intruding, but they made me feel right at home that very first day. We sat in the dining room for over an hour after dinner and talked about a lot of things. Steve's dad and I discussed theology for a while, and I was amazed at how much he knew. Steve had told me that his dad never went to college, but he explained to me that he had read everything he could get his hands on. The man's knowledge of Scripture was amazing. After dessert, Chrissy and I headed up to the garage, with me partially leaning on her for support. I was still weak from my stay in the hospital, and wasn't able to get around totally on my own.

We got into the small apartment, and much to my surprise, there was a shower up there as well. Christina and I took turns using the shower and getting ready for bed. It would be the first night we spent together. We were both tired from the events of the day. We lay in bed together, and just held each other all night. I woke in the middle of the night and watched her sleeping. Her face had a peaceful expression, and with the moonbeams coming in the window and lighting up her face, it seemed almost like a movie. I could hear her breathe, and I wondered what she was dreaming that was making her smile.

The next morning, I went out with Christina and Steve to look for a car for us. It would be primarily Christina's for a little while, at least until I was strong enough to get around. We had found a Toyota Corolla advertised in the paper that morning, and we had enough money to pay for it clean and clear. We drove down to the house of the person advertising the car, and took it out for a spin. Christina loved it, and was thrilled at the prospect of having such a car. We decided to buy the car, and drove back to the house in a nice little car. We were still waiting for the insurance check to come in for us.

Christina loved driving the car back and forth to work. It was the first car she ever had, and I was more than happy to let her have the car. We took the car shopping on days she was off to buy necessities for when we left. With Christmas approaching, we prepared to take our leave of Memphis. Mike and the folks at work had prepared a wedding party for us, which would be taking place the Saturday before Christmas break. Steve's parents and members of his church were coming too, one of the ladies had her own cake shop and was making us a wedding cake. We were going to do a "church wedding" with the party, and have pictures taken to remember such a special time in our lives. When that Friday came, Christina was so excited that she could barely contain herself. She was thrilled at the thought of finally leaving Memphis. And she was excited over the big party the next day. Mike had gone ahead and rented the entire restaurant for the day, so we would have it all to ourselves.

That Saturday, Chrissy didn't have to work, so we spent the day out car shopping. We settled on a minivan with wood paneling. I called it the dork-mobile, but Christina thought I was being harsh with that nickname. But it was big enough to hold all of our stuff, and I knew it would work for what we needed to do.

That night, we got together at the restaurant with everybody. After it had closed down, everybody had come in and decorated the restaurant with wedding stuff. The girls 'ooohed and aahed' over the various gifts that they gave Christina, and several of the guys had brought me some tools as a guy's wedding present. Mike and Steve had chipped in and bought me a new Bible and commentary set. I got everybody's address, and promised to write after we got where we were going. As we prepared to leave, Mike came walking up and shook my hand.

"Jason, I just wanted to let you know, that no matter what that college thinks, you're one of the best Christians I've ever known. You're a good guy, and I know you'll do well."

Christina and I hopped into the van, and drove back to Steve's place. We stayed the night, and went to morning services with Steve's family one last time the next morning. That afternoon, we drove off.

Chapter Sixteen:
Starting Over

As we drove off, we were both taking separate cars. I had bought us some walkie-talkies from the local electronics store so we didn't have to use up our cell phone minutes on the trip calling back and forth to each other. We drove toward Ohio until we came to a rest stop, and there I dialed Sarah's number to let her know we were coming. The phone seemed to ring forever, and then on came her voice mail. I was already prepared to leave a message for her, but the message she had for me left me stunned.

Hey, this is Sarah's phone! Jason, you're the only one with this number, so I know it's you calling me. I heard about your accident, and I'm sorry you were hurt. I hope you're doing better and that you and Christina are doing well. I'm not sure how to tell you this, I guess the blunt way is the best way to go. I left the girl's home. There's a couple in town that helped me to escape. So I'm on my own now, moving from place to place to try and keep away from Mom and Dad. Anyway, I've started seeing a guy in the new town I'm in. He's older . . . okay, a lot older. But he's a good guy Jason. Someday I hope you'll get a chance to meet him. I've found work out here, and I have my own apartment.

It's small but cozy. I'm turning off this phone soon, so you'll not be able to get a hold of me for a while. But I promise you, when I get settled and on my feet solidly, I'll find you. Be good big brother!

I hung up the phone in shock and looked at Christina.

"She left already."

"What?!" said Christina in a mixture of shock and disbelief, "She's already gone?"

"Yes, apparently, somebody helped her escape the home." I responded.

Christina and I sat down on a bench and I relayed to her what the message said. We talked about this sudden twist of fate for a few moments, and then decided to take off again. This time, we turned our vehicles south toward North Carolina. I called Dave up on our way and let him know we'd be there a day or two early. I had been emailing Dave back and forth, making arrangements to get down there to where he was. Dave had found some work for me, and a place for us to live. His church was a good Independent Fundamental Baptist church, one a little more balanced than what I had grown up around.

Christina and I found a motel room to stay the night at instead of driving throughout the cold, dark night. We ate over at a small country kitchen, then went back to our room. For the first time since we'd been married, we were all alone. When we opened the door to the room, I surprised Christina by scooping her off her feet and walking her in through the doorway. She laughed and giggled as I carried her in the room, and I left her inside while I secured the vehicles and brought in our night bags with our change of clothes.

I woke up well before it was time for our wake up call, and looked over at Christina. She always smiled in her sleep, and again I found myself wondering what she was dreaming about. I reached over and brushed her hair out of her beautiful face and softly kissed her cheek.

When morning came, we got all cleaned up and ready for the road. We had devotions, then walked over to a breakfast buffet and had some food. Then we hopped into our cars and took off again for Dave's town.

When we approached the North Carolina border, I gave Dave a call again to let him know we were near. Dave lived not too far from the border. He gave us directions, and within a couple hours we were pulling into his driveway. He came walking out of the house with a big smile on his face.

"Hey guys! How are you doing?" Dave said.

"Doing well, how about you?" I responded.

"I'm doing well," he said, "come on inside, mom and dad are dying to meet you two."

We walked inside the house chattering as we went. Dave's parents made us feel right at home, and peppered us with multiple questions about our trip and our time at college. We laughed and talked until after dinner. We stayed the night there with them, and the next morning, Dave took us out to our new house. The air was turning cold as we got out at the small house. Dave told us it was getting ready to snow, and as we started getting our stuff out of the cars, the snow began.

Chapter Seventeen:
Christina Speaks

The snow was falling all around us as we started unpacking everything. Growing up in Memphis, I never had seen snow much, and certainly not like this. It was sticking to the ground, and piling deeper as we struggled to get everything in the house. I was completely enamored by the snow, where Jason was just bothered by it. He had seen snow enough in his life he explained, and wasn't that thrilled by the sight of all that white stuff on the ground.

When we finished getting everything inside the house, Dave left us to get settled in on our own. Jason and I spent over an hour getting the house set up how we wanted everything. He let me do all the decorating, and I enjoyed putting everything up just how I liked. Dave told us of a place in town to get our pictures developed, and drew us directions to Jason's new job he would be working. We were excited about our new town and home. We made plans to go into town in the morning, and get our pictures developed.

Jason put a cd into our stereo. It was playing a mixture of Christmas and Classical music. I walked out to the front porch and watched the snowflakes falling while listening to the music play in the background. Jason followed me out after a minute and put a jacket around my shoulders. I wrapped myself in it, and felt Jason wrap his arms around me and we watched the snow come down together.

I walked off the porch, and out into the snow and let it fall all around me. It was exciting for me to stick my tongue out into the cold air and catch a snowflake on my tongue. Jason laughed as he watched me twirling in the snow. I grabbed a pile of snow to make a snowball and threw it at him. He laughed, and jumped down in the snow to follow suit. I started running, and he chased me. I squealed as he caught me and lifted me off my feet.

Then he set me back down on the ground and we kissed. I never had felt any happier than I did right at this moment. Everything in the world felt right again, and Jason had put it all back together for me. We could still hear the sounds of the stereo playing, and Moonlight Sonata came on, filling the air with a beautiful sound as the dark night approached. Jason grabbed my hand, and we began dancing in the snow to the music. It all seemed so surreal, to have come from such a horrible place, and now to be surrounded by this wonderland of white. As we spun around, I knew without a doubt that we would be together forever, and happiness was our reward.

Chapter Eighteen:

Sarah

I woke up feeling the cold wind blast through my blanket. It was still dark out, but I had no idea what time it was. I picked up my poor excuse for a blanket and wrapped it around myself and huddled close to the wall I had chosen for shelter. I was living on the street now, and little things I had taken for granted like shelter I now longed for.

When I left the girl's home, I found myself in the company of a much older man, twenty years my senior. He was charming and witty, and even though I thought I had grown out of being so naive, I still fell for the lies he told me. He had helped me find an apartment, and was paying my rent while I worked a low paying job to make extra money for things I wanted.

This arrangement worked well only for a couple of weeks. Then one night I came home from work and he was in the apartment. He started out first just talking with me, then he revealed the true purpose of his visit. I was shocked at first, and then told him to leave. He began threatening to throw me out on the streets if I didn't give him what he wanted. I tried to reason with him, but he wouldn't hear me. He grabbed me and threw me against the wall. My head hit a sharp corner, and I became disoriented and unable to move or defend myself. Later that night, I found myself out on the streets with just the things I had come to town with, and the little bit of money I had in my purse.

My first thought had been to call Jason, but I didn't want him to know that I had failed at being out on my own. And I was ashamed because of what happened. Now, I was sleeping on the street, and finding food from wherever I could.

Detroit was a cold city in the winter, and the wind was blowing bitterly tonight. I decided to walk down to the McDonald's, and buy myself a cup of coffee with some of the change I had. McDonald's had a policy against loitering, but as long as I had some coffee, I could stay inside for a few minutes and get warm. The coffee was really warm, and I sat in the back of the restaurant and sipped it as I looked outside at the cars going past.

When my time in the restaurant was up, I got a refill and went back out onto the streets. I could see the sun coming up, and buses coming into the city to take children to school. I could feel a tear forming in my eye as I remembered what it was like to be young and innocent. How I wished I could be again.

When the sun finally came up, I decided to find myself a better place to sleep. The loading dock where I had slept the night before hadn't offered much protection. I walked through the city, looking at all the decorations. Christmas was almost here, and for the first time in my life, I was going to be totally alone on Christmas day. It was a bittersweet feeling looking at all the people carrying gifts and seeing the wreaths hung up everywhere.

I passed by a homeless shelter, and looked at all the people crowded inside. There were several men standing outside inviting people to come in, and handing out Christian tracts. I took one and shoved it in my pocket and continued on my way. "I've had enough of religion," I thought bitterly to myself, "what do I need this crap for?" There was a place nearby that helped homeless people out by giving work for the day that payed cash, so I went there to get some money.

I was paired with another girl, and we were given work sorting mail in the basement of a business. We talked as the day went on, sharing our stories about how we came to be on the streets. She told me that her name was Veronica, and that her dad and mom had raised her on the streets, and she didn't really know anything else. The little bit of money she was making at this job was going to be saved, and she'd try to get herself a motel room for the night every now and then. She told me sometimes she'd go to the missions for the night and to get some warm food, and invited me to go with her that night. Reluctantly, I accepted her offer. I suppose I accepted mostly at the thought of a warm meal. It would be nice for a change, instead of the cold food I was finding outside the restaurants.

After the job was finished, we went and picked up our money, which amounted to about $35 for a days work. We both walked down to the mission together, but fortunately it wasn't the same one I passed by earlier. This one was a little smaller it seemed from the look of the place. We went inside and they directed us up to the showers. While we showered, they took our clothes and ran them through the wash to clean them all up. We were given a set of clothes to wear at the mission. Downstairs, they had a spaghetti meal waiting for us, which we both gulped down greedily.

Veronica told me that in the morning we would get breakfast too, and could take some food with us. After dinner, they had devotions up in the chapel that we were required to attend in order to stay the night. Veronica listened intently while I flipped through the songbook in front of me. This wasn't the kind of preaching I was accustomed to, and some of the songs I had never heard before. I guess they were the modern songs preachers had always warned us about. After the service was over, we started to head upstairs, when one of the older lady workers pulled me aside for a moment.

"Hello there, is this your first time here?" she asked.

"Yes ma'am, it's my first time here." I said, feeling a little awkward.

"Would you mind sitting and talking with me for a few minutes?"

"I guess so," I responded.

"So, what's your name?"

"Sarah" I said looking at her.

"Well Sarah, how is it you ended up here tonight?"

"Um, Veronica invited me to come with her."

"Well, what I meant was, how is it you ended up on the streets?"

I could see that she was genuinely interested and curious, but I didn't want to talk about the matter that awful much.

"I'd rather not talk about that right now," I said.

"Well that's okay," she said, "we don't have to talk about it if you don't want. I thought you were new when I first saw you. I noticed you didn't seem interested in the sermon, do you mind talking about that?"

"I'm not really into church any more."

"Oh," she said looking at me sadly, "Is that something you'd rather not talk about as well?"

"Yes ma'am."

"Okay then, well, if you ever need to talk, you just ask for Miss Andrews okay?"

"Yes ma'am, I will."

With that, I went back upstairs and joined Veronica in the ladies room where we would sleep for the night. We were provided with a nightgown to sleep in, and I closed my eyes and quickly fell asleep. The next morning, we went down to breakfast, where they provided us with pancakes and fresh fruit for our meal. Veronica and I both stuffed some of the fruit into our pockets so we would have food for later. We walked down the street for a while, to look and see if there would be any more work today, but there wasn't. So we walked around the city. It was a much colder day, and after a couple hours of walking, Veronica and I split up, agreeing to meet on Monday at the same place to get some work.

I found myself in an alley, huddled up against a laundry vent for some heat from the dryer. I could see pairs of young men go by. Dressed up in ties, going around knocking on doors. From the way they talked, I determined that they were from an Independent Baptist church. I hoped they would ignore me, and they did. They walked by me several times, taking care to walk on the other side of the alley and avoid eye contact. After sitting there for a couple hours, I got up and left the alley. I decided to walk down to McDonald's again and get some coffee.

McDonald's was full of young men like what I had been seeing all day, and several young women too that looked like they were from the same place. I grabbed my coffee and went and sat in the back of the restaurant and watched them all laughing and talking. I remembered what it was like to be like they were now. As I sat there drinking my coffee, I looked outside the window, and felt my stomach knot up. It was snowing now, and I didn't know how to find a good shelter from the snow. I grabbed my coffee and ran out of the restaurant to try and find a place to sleep. After searching for half an hour, I found a large cardboard box in the back of an alley. I took the box and moved it onto a loading dock and huddled up inside of it for warmth. My breath quickly heated the box up to a cozy temperature, and now I realized why I always saw other homeless using a box to sleep in at night. I laid myself down, and second week in a row I cried myself to sleep.

Chapter Nineteen:
Jason and Christina Settle In

The day after getting settled in our house, Christina and I drove into town to get some necessities for the house. We stopped off at the drugstore first to get our film developed. Then we drove down to the grocery story to get stocked up. I let Christina do most of the shopping, since she apparently didn't approve of my suggestion of fish sticks and ramen noodles.

Christina bought way too many vegetables for my liking, but I had decided that whatever she cooked, I was at least going to try. Even if it did kill me. After we finished shopping for our groceries, we drove back to the drugstore to pick up our pictures. The entire ride back home, Christina picked through the pictures and giggled. Every now and then she'd show me one that she especially liked.

When we got back to the house, I was surprised at how cold it had gotten inside. Of course, it didn't help that I had left the heater off. So while we waited on the heater to warm up, Christina and I cuddled up on the couch together and watched a video.

When the video was over, Christina began making dinner while I went out to bring some firewood in the house. The place we were renting had both electric heat, and a fireplace. I had already decided to use the fireplace as a primary heat source while we were awake, and the electric heat for when we were asleep or out. Christina thought the fireplace was more romantic anyway. I just saw it as a cheap source of heat. Dave had gotten us a cord of wood before we got there, and put it all right by the front porch so we wouldn't have to walk far to get the wood. I brought in a couple of arm loads, and then stacked more beside the front door for later, so if Christina ever had to run out for some it would be easier on her.

After dinner, we got dressed and ready for the midweek service at Dave's church. We took Christina's car to the church, which was only about three miles down the road. It was a small church, much smaller than either Memphis Metro, or the church I had grown up with. We were immediately made to feel welcome by everybody there, and it seemed that everybody made it a special point to introduce themselves to us.

Christina and I enjoyed the service. The teaching time was about the Sermon on the Mount, and for the first time in several years, I felt like I had listened to a real sermon that I could apply to my life. I could tell that I was going to like this church. After the service, the pastor gave us a copy of the church's constitution and statement of faith for us to go over together before deciding to join the church. The entire way home, Christina and I talked about how much we enjoyed the service.

Over the course of the next few weeks, Christina and I got more settled into our new home. We were enjoying our new church, and my job was going great. I had begun taking some correspondence classes to keep up with my education. We were starting to get over the excitement of being in a new location, but were still very much excited about the fact that we were now married.

I had continued to try and call Sarah, but to no avail. She never answered, and after a few calls, her cell phone had been turned off. I worried about her, and wondered where she was and how she was doing. I had also written to mom and dad hoping they had some news regarding Sarah, but they never returned any letters or calls. They were angry, and I knew and accepted that fact.

One day, I got a call from Christina while I was at work, and she was complaining about being sick. After work, I dropped by the drug store and picked up some medicine for her. She looked miserable when I got home, and was glad to get some medicine.

"You feeling any better Chrissy?" I asked as I leaned over to kiss her forehead.

"No," she responded, "not really. I'm still feeling really lousy."

"Well, I'll take care of dinner tonight, you just lay back and relax."

I walked into the kitchen and began doing some cooking. Christina loved green beans and chicken, so I grabbed some chicken breast and rice to make a stir-fry. I had some green beans sizzling in a pan soon as well, and a few minutes later Christina joined me in the kitchen for dinner. We talked for a little while about how the day had gone, and after dinner I cleaned up while she went in the family room and read a book. She went to bed early that night because she still felt a little ill, so I stayed up studying alone.

Over the next few days, Christina was still feeling sick. I mostly attributed it to the change in the climate, and supposed that the sudden shift from a mild winter to cold weather had caused her to get the flu. I bought her some more medicine from the drug store toward the end of the week since she still wasn't feeling better, but when the weekend was over she was still sick.

Chapter Twenty:

Christmas in Detroit

I still wasn't finding any way out of my situation in Detroit. Living in a cardboard box wasn't how I had pictured things turning out for me. Veronica and I were still meeting up for work and sometimes staying at the shelter together. We talked about all kinds of things when we were together, and I began sharing my story with her and sweet old Miss Andrews at the shelter one night.

"They really sent you off to a girl's home?" asked Miss Andrews in shock.

"Yes ma'am," I replied, "I guess they didn't know what to do to help me."

"But still," interrupted Veronica, "it's their job to look after you and help and protect you. Not just ship you off to some home when things get hard."

"That's not the way things worked out for me I guess." I responded.

"What was it like there for you?" asked Veronica.

"I hated it, we had to be up by 7am every morning to do our chores, then we had school, chapel, and then more chores. We had some time to ourselves, but they always said that 'idle hands were the devil's workshop,' so we stayed busy all the time."

"Was it strict there?" inquired Miss Andrews.

"Very strict. We weren't allowed to do much of anything, and if we disobeyed we got in a lot of trouble."

"Can you give some examples for us?"

"Well, like, when I first got there, I didn't like getting up early in the morning. So I would still be in bed after the time to get up. Well, after letting me get away with it for a few days, they finally decided to punish me. I spent three days in a room by myself and wasn't allowed to talk to anybody. They'd bring me food, but I couldn't do anything. And then they played sermons over the speakers in the room all day long."

"They really did that to you?" asked Veronica, "I mean, why would they do that to somebody? That sounds like something people to do prisoners of war."

"That's awful," said Miss Andrews, "I can't believe somebody would do that to you."

When we finished talking, Miss Andrews gave me a great big hug. "Don't blame God for what those people did to you sweetie. They don't represent God or the church no matter what they say. That's not real Christianity."

I just nodded my head, but her words didn't have much meaning to me inside. I still felt as empty and hollow as I always had. At this time in my life, nothing mattered much to me anymore, other than trying to survive. Before bed that night, I told Veronica about my brother Jason.

"Why don't you go to him?" she asked, "It sounds like he would be willing to take you in."

"Yeah, but he just got married, I don't want to be in the way."

"I don't think he'd see it that way Sarah," she said, "I think he'd be happy to see you again."

"Maybe," I said.

The memories of the girls home haunted me as I tried to sleep that night. I could have told so much more of my story than I had, but it was too much to talk about. I still had visible scars from the things that had happened there. I didn't want to be reminded any more than necessary about what had gone on at that place.

When Christmas day came, I bundled myself up and went down to the city hall to look at the Christmas tree they had on display. I sat on some stairs looking at it while I relived happy memories from Christmases that were a long time gone. After sitting there for what seemed like only a few minutes, a police officer came along and told me loitering wasn't permitted, and I had to move along. I walked through some of the nicer sections of the city, and could hear the excited laughter of children who had gotten Christmas presents that they were excited about. Some children were playing with their new gifts on the sidewalks, and I smiled as I watched them run around showing off their toys.

Christmas day came and with nothing special for me. For the first time, I was really starting to miss Jason, and I thought about calling him up. I had his number in my pocket, and I found myself standing by a phone booth late one night. I looked at the number, and picked up the phone. I stared at the phone for a few moments and started to dial the number. Then fear got the best of me, and I slammed the phone back down. I ran back out into the night and made my way back to my alley. I didn't want Jason to know how much trouble I was in, and I felt almost certain that he wouldn't help me now.

Chapter Twenty-One:
Christina's Surprise

I was still sick after Christmas, and couldn't seem to shake it for more than a day or so at a time. Jason was concerned, and was talking about sending me to a doctor to find out what was wrong. I didn't want to go to the doctor, but Jason was becoming more insistent as the symptoms failed to disappear.

I had been a victim of colds and pneumonia before, but this felt like something else entirely to me. I wasn't sure about what it was, but I had an idea.

Jason and I were still enjoying church very much. He was

teaching a Sunday school class now, as well as taking classes over the internet. I was constantly amazed by his ability to juggle so many things at once. He was working at least forty hours a week, if not fifty. And he was studying and preparing lessons for Sunday. I didn't know how he managed to do it and still have time for me.

After a couple of days, I went down to the drugstore to buy a home pregnancy kit. I didn't tell Jason, because I didn't want to get him excited for nothing. I sat and waited the prescribed number of minutes, then checked the results. I looked at the test, which read that I was positive. I felt my heart jump in my throat. "I'm going to be a mommy," I thought. I decided I would wait to tell Jason, until I was absolutely sure. I made a call to a local doctor to set up an appointment for the next day.

The next morning, Jason went to work like normal, while I got ready for my visit to the doctor. When I got there, the nurse handed me what seemed like an endless amount of paperwork to fill out. A few times I had to call Jason to get his help with answering a question. When the doctor finally saw me, he listened to me describe the symptoms, then he brought in a nurse to have some tests done. The doctor left for a while, while I waited nervously for him to come back and tell me what was happening.

The doctor came back in the room after what seemed like an eternity. He had a sheet of papers in his hand, and he looked at them and then at me.

"Well Mrs. Tate, I'm going to say in about seven months this will all be over," he said with a grin, "it seems that you are now expecting Mrs Tate."

I stared at him in shock for a moment. "I'm really pregnant?" I asked.

"Yes ma'am, that's the diagnosis. I'm guessing that you're about a month and a half to two months pregnant at this point."

I smiled and looked at the doctor, "So about seven months until the baby is here?"

"Yes ma'am. Now, I'd like to go ahead and begin scheduling some more appointments with you now, so we can take care of you and the baby right up to the point that the baby comes. You'll need to see me every so often while you're pregnant to make sure everything goes smoothly. The receptionist will set up a new appointment with you and give you a pamphlet of things to expect at this point in the pregnancy. You can go ahead and get dressed and go on out now."

"Thank you," I said still beaming, "thank you very much!"

He smiled, "Not a problem Mrs Tate, I hope to see you again soon."

I went home and my first impulse was to call up Jason. But I resisted that impulse, I would tell him when he came home. Instead, I sat on the couch and began reading the pamphlet the doctor had given me. I read, and reread it while I waited for Jason to come home. After a couple of hours, I heard his car pull into the driveway.

Jason came in the door, and looked over at me. "So what'd the doctor say?"

"Well, he figured out what it is I've got," I said, "He gave me this pamphlet on it and set up another appointment for me in a couple of weeks."

I saw a flash of concern in Jason's eyes as he walked over to look at the pamphlet and for a moment I felt guilty for teasing him this way.

He looked at the pamphlet for a minute and I could see it sinking in for him. "You're pregnant?" he asked in shocked disbelief.

I laughed, "Yes, we're expecting now."

He jumped up from the couch and pulled me up with him. He grabbed me and lifted me off my feet and spun me around and we both laughed. Then he set me down and kiss me. He put his hand on my belly, and looked into my eyes.

"Well, this is definitely better than the flu," he said with a grin.

I laughed, "Yes, it definitely is. I'm so excited!"

Jason and I spent the rest of the night talking excitedly about what we wanted to do to get ready for the baby. I was happy to see how excited he was. It sent a thrill through me to know that he was as excited as me at the prospect of being a parent. We fell asleep on the couch that night. I woke in the morning to find a blanket wrapped around me and Jason in the kitchen making breakfast. We ate together before Jason left for work. I spent the rest of the day flipping through baby books and magazines. We were going to be parents, and for me this was something greater than anything else that had happened to us. I couldn't imagine a better life.

Chapter Twenty-Two:
Full Circle

Sarah stumbled her way through the streets of Detroit. The winter was not being kind to her, and her body was wracked with an illness she didn't know how to handle. Coffee was not able to warm her any longer, and her makeshift shelter wasn't keeping out the bitter wind. She had awoken early in the morning and decided to head toward Veronica's place. Maybe Veronica and Miss Andrews would be able to help her. She staggered her way through the alleys. When she approached Veronica's place, she tried to call out for help, but her voice didn't come. Sarah fell to the ground and her whole world went black.

The phone rang at six in the morning, I rolled over and looked at the clock before picking up. The number was out of state, and I didn't recognize it as anyone I knew. I picked it up and answered.

"Hello," I mumbled only half awake.

"Hello, this is the Detroit Police calling, we found your number on the person of a young woman who was taken to the hospital earlier this morning. We were wondering if maybe you could help us find out who she is."

I swung myself up out of bed, "Does she have blonde hair? About eighteen years old?"

By now Christina was awake and tapped on my arm wanting to know what was going on. I motioned for her to wait as I listened to the police describe the girl they were talking about. It was definitely Sarah.

"Yes, that's Sarah, my sister." I said to the officer after he finished describing her.

"Okay, well, are you or your parents going to be able to come and take her home or to where you live? Or is there someone up here we should contact?"

"I'll take care of it officer," I responded, "I'll be up there as soon as I can."

The officer gave me some more information on who to get in touch with when I got to Detroit, and I hurriedly wrote it down. When I hung up, I began explaining everything to Christina.

"Do you want me to go up with you?" She asked.

"Yeah," I said, "I'm getting ready to call up work and tell them I'll need a couple of personal days off. We'll gas up the van and head up north after that. And I'll need to call Dave to ask him to watch the house."

An hour later we were on the road to Michigan. After driving all day, we finally arrived in Detroit and found St. John's hospital. When we got inside, we asked for Dr. Philips, who was Sarah's attending physician. When he finally came down, he explained to us that Sarah had pneumonia, and she was fairly ill. But in a couple of days we'd probably be able to transport her down to North Carolina. We went up to her room, and found a couple of other people in there already. They introduced themselves as Veronica and Miss Mary Andrews. Christina spoke with the two of them out in the hall as I spoke to Sarah.

"Hey little sis." I said, taking her hand in mine. "How are you feeling tonight?"

"Tired." She said weakly.

"Yeah, I'll bet you are tired. Hopefully in a couple days we'll get you down to North Carolina with us and you can recuperate there. What do you think of that?"

"I think I'd like that." She said.

I could tell she was exhausted. Her eyelids were heavy, and her breathing was ragged.

"Well sis, I'll come back and visit you tomorrow. You need to rest tonight."

She nodded her head weakly, and her eyes closed as she

147

drifted off to sleep.

Christina and I went out to find a hotel after having dinner with Veronica and Miss Andrews. I was a little troubled later that night as I thought about what the two had told me about Sarah. Christina and I talked for a while about helping Sarah get on her feet back home. We called mom and dad and left them a message but never got a response from them.

A couple of days later, we were all three on the road back to North Carolina again. Sarah lay in the backseat, sleeping for most of the trip. Christina and I switched back and forth between driving for the trip home.

When we got back home, I carried Sarah inside and set her down in the guest bedroom. Dave and his family had brought over a twin bed for Sarah so she would have somewhere to sleep. After we got her settled in and unpacked, I went to talk to Sarah.

"So how you feeling today?" I asked.

"I'm feeling better." She said.

"You feel like talking about Detroit?"

I could see the tears begin to well up in her eyes. She began telling me everything that happened to her. From the first day she had left the girls home, to the day I had come to the hospital. I listened to her and Christina joined us after a few minutes and sat beside Sarah on the bed. Christina held Sarah as she cried during parts of the story. Sarah also told us about some of the things that had gone on at the girls home, as well as the stories about her time in Detroit.

Over the next few weeks, Sarah and I got to know each other

better than we had before. It became obvious to me that Sarah no longer had any interest in God or the Bible at all. It wasn't that she didn't believe in God, she just couldn't bring herself to put any faith in Him after what had happened to her, done supposedly in the name of God. Any faith she might have had was now gone.

Sarah and Christina were spending a lot of time together and getting one of the rooms ready for the baby that was on the way. They had already decided on a neutral color to paint the room so we wouldn't have to repaint if the baby was a different sex than expected. Sarah was helping to cook now, since Christina was having a little trouble getting up to cook in the mornings.

Sarah was working a job at the local convenience store that was right around the corner. Her interests were quickly becoming quite different from ours, and after hanging out with us for a few months, she decided to move. She bought a car, and got her stuff together to move out west to Texas. She had found a job in Houston, and an apartment that was cheap enough for her.

And now it was just Christina and myself. The baby was only a couple months away, and so far it had been smooth sailing. The night Sarah left, Christina and I curled up on the couch together and watched the sunset together. Even though Sarah no longer believed, I knew everything would turn out all right. I had Christina, and our baby was almost here as well. My life would be full. Though the Destroyer had come to take away our happiness, he'd not succeeded. I had my faith, and I had my Christina. And as she whispered in my ear one night as we danced, "happiness was our reward."